PENGUIN BOOKS

RUMOR!

Hal Morgan was born in 1954 and graduated
from Hampshire College. He is the author of
Big Time: American Tall-Tale Postcards, and
co-author of *Amazing 3-D* and *Prairie Fires
and Paper Moons: The American Photographic
Postcard, 1900–1920.* Kerry Tucker was born
in Connecticut in 1955, raised in Youngstown,
Ohio, and educated at Chatham College in
Pittsburgh. She is the author of two other
books, *Greetings from New York: A Visit to
Manhattan in Postcards* and *Greetings from
Los Angeles: A Visit to the City of Angels in
Postcards.* She now divides her time between
writing and law studies. Morgan and Tucker
previously collaborated on *The Shower Song-
book.* Together they run Steam Press, a book
production company in Cambridge, Massachusetts.

RUMOR!

Hal Morgan and
Kerry Tucker

A Steam Press Book

PENGUIN BOOKS

Penguin Books Ltd., Harmondsworth,
Middlesex, England
Penguin Books, 40 West 23rd Street,
New York, New York 10010, U.S.A.
Penguin Books Australia Ltd., Ringwood,
Victoria, Australia
Penguin Books Canada Limited, 2801 John Street,
Markham, Ontario, Canada L3R 1B4
Penguin Books (N.Z.) Ltd. 182–190 Wairau Road,
Auckland 10, New Zealand

First published 1984

Printed in the United States of America by
Fairfield Graphics, Fairfield, Pennsylvania
Set in Century Schoolbook
Design and production by Steam Press,
Cambridge, Massachusetts

ISBN: 0-14-007036-2

"The sky is falling!"–*Chicken Little*

INTRODUCTION

WE REMEMBER when Paul McCartney died. Wendy Kessler broke the news to us. She was disconsolate; we were astounded. John's voice said *what* on the record? When you played it *backwards*? After school we crouched beside our hi-fis, squealing in agony at the grotesque voice we were sure we could hear at the end of "Strawberry Fields Forever." "I . . . buried . . . Paul . . ." it said, and we mourned. He was so young and so *cute*. Why did God take *him* instead of Ringo?

Why did anyone believe that rumor? We loved Paul. Why did we want to think he was dead? Maybe the rumor was seductive simply because it was so elaborate. The clues were everywhere: in the lyrics, in the photographs on the backs of the albums, in the lettering on the cover, in the Beatles' clothes, in their gestures, and on their license plates. It was a strange and habit-forming mystery game, and we somehow felt on the "inside" because we knew the clues.

Is that it? Is it the promise of "insideness" that compels people to gather and spread silly and fantastic—even destructive—stories about celebrities and products? That appears to be the only explanation for some widely believed rumors. Other rumors seem to spring from hopes of wish fulfillment, like all the stories about getting something for nothing—a new Ford for a 1943 copper penny; new motorcycles for fabulously low prices if you write to a special address; big dollars for fingernail clippings; or, for the more altruistic—seeing-eye dogs in exchange for gum-wrapper chains.

Another brand of rumor breeds with monstrous speed in times of disaster and emergency; apparently when normal channels of information fail to operate, people fabricate their own news. The United States was so tormented by rumors during World War II—that the army was dumping food in the ocean; that the Japanese were invading Oregon—that several major newspapers maintained "rumor clinics" for the purpose of setting people straight. The rumors that plagued San Francisco just after the cataclysmic earthquake of 1906 were more than macabre; one story had it that the quake had set the animals from the San Francisco Zoo free and that they were roaming Golden Gate Park, eating refugees encamped there. Today emergency workers recognize the possibility of rumors as the volatile by-product of any disaster, and most cities include rumor-information centers as part of their routine plans for dealing with crises.

Rumors that attach themselves to a specific product

have been the bane of manufacturers since the industrial revolution. Once started they are practically impossible to trace, but a rumor from the twenties that aluminum cookware poisoned food has been firmly attributed to one man's personal vendetta against the metal. Every time a product rumor becomes popular, another rumor rides its coattails—that the damaging rumor was started by a competitor. Companies have been known to use tactics like these, and at one time several rumor-mongering firms blatantly advertised their services. The best-known rumor service, W. Howard Downey and Associates, was established in 1915 and had offices in four cities. The company, which claimed to be able to introduce a rumor anywhere in the country on only a few hours' notice, usually went about its dirty business by dispatching two-man teams to crowded places—most often trains and buses—where they would pretend to strike up conversations, but would actually ignite rumors.

Such firms are now illegal, of course, and rumor patterns of recent years have shown just how perilous it could be for a company to launch a rumor about the competition. Rumors have strong tendencies to jump the track; the spider eggs that were reputed to be in bubble gum one year were said to be in fast-food hamburgers the next. If rumors move as erratically as that, it is clearly risky business to point one at a competing brand—the chances of it boomeranging are enormous.

Other rumors seem to serve a "cautionary" purpose—like the story that Jean Harlow died from peroxide buildup on her scalp; or that one woman so neglected her beehive hairdo that a black widow spider moved into it; or that a group of teenagers took LSD and then stared at the sun until their eyeballs fried. The message in these rumors is clear: don't bleach your hair; don't tease it either; and don't take drugs. Rumors like these are probably started by parents.

Some rumors are clearly the work of paranoids, like the rumor that fluoridation is a Communist plot; or that certain companies are owned by devil worshipers; or that—travesty of travesties—the astronauts never really went to the moon at all. People who start rumors like these are just nuts.

And then there are all those rumors that simply defy categorization—like the one that Ritz crackers have the word "sex" microscopically embossed all over them; or that Dwight Eisenhower had a rendezvous with space aliens. Who dreams these up? Why? Nobody knows. Maybe people spread them just to see the incredulous looks on other people's faces.

Rumors—fickle, inane, and baffling as they can be—have earned their place in American folklore. At their worst, they reflect the fears and prejudices of our culture; at their best, they take us for a walk on the country's wacky side.

We know that many of you will be disappointed to

learn that Humphrey Bogart wasn't really the model for the Gerber baby and that Mr. Greenjeans isn't really Frank Zappa's father. We're sorry. That's another strange thing about rumors. Many otherwise clear-minded people often want the most ridiculous things to be true.

★ ★ Rudolph Valentino died from eating food prepared in aluminum cookware. (1926)

Not true. This was one of the many rumors about the dangers of aluminum that circulated in the twenties. Early versions told of hundreds of cases of food poisoning caused by aluminum cookware. Next came the story that three Navy seamen had been poisoned by eating oysters stored in aluminum pots—the Navy was said to be responding by destroying all its aluminum cooking equipment. As the rumors gained momentum, they told of aluminum-caused cancer and infantile paralysis and culminated with the death of Rudolph Valentino.

Valentino actually died of peritonitis caused by a perforated ulcer; the death had nothing to do with aluminum. The rumors had everything to do with one Howard J. Force, who made his living selling anti-aluminum pamphlets to the public and to the makers of non-aluminum cookware. As a sideline, Force also sold a bogus anti-cancer drug called "Pheno-Isolin," which presumably was bought by the terrified readers of the pamphlets.

A related rumor attributed Jean Harlow's death in 1937 to peroxide buildup on her scalp. The story probably made thousands of would-be blondes think twice before bleaching, but it wasn't true. The actress died of uremic poisoning.

★ ★ A leper was found working in the Chesterfield cigarette factory in Richmond, Virginia. (1934)

Not true. Wild as this story sounds, it spread rapidly and cost Ligget & Meyers, the manufacturer, thousands of dollars in lost business. Because it followed on the heels of another tale—that the company had contributed half a million dollars to the war chest of Adolf Hitler—Ligget & Meyers suspected foul play. The two rumors coming so close together—and the fact that they so obviously benefited competing cigarette brands at Chesterfield's expense—led Ligget & Meyers to launch an investigation. Concentrating on the leper story, the company hired detectives and offered thousand-dollar rewards to the first twenty-five people to give evidence leading to the rumor's source. In the wording of the reward offer, the company made it clear that they fully expected their search to end in the board room of a competitor: "We do not object to legitimate competition, but cowardly attacks of this sort have no place in American business or American life."

But rumors are slippery beasts and are not often easy to pin down. After weeks of interviewing friends of friends and chasing down *their* friends and neighbors and dentists, the trackers finally gave up the search. They would probably have given up much sooner if they had realized how old their quarry really was; the legend of the leper-in-the-factory had, by 1934, been making the rounds of tobacco plants and food processors for more than a hundred years. He may show up yet again.

★ ★ The song "Gloomy Sunday," recorded by Paul Whiteman, was banned from radio broadcasts because it had trig-
gered so many suicides. (1936)

Partly true. The original Hungarian version of the song,
written by composer Rezso Seress and lyricist Laszlo Javor,
ran into some trouble with the Budapest police after a series
of mysterious deaths. Written in 1933, the song played without undo publicity or success until early 1936, when a Budapest shoemaker named Joseph Keller left a suicide note
that included lyrics from the ballad. A police investigation
turned up seventeen other suicides inspired by the piece—
two committed after hearing it played by a gypsy band, others
after listening to recorded versions, and a few who had taken
their lives while holding the sheet music. Budapest author-
ities banned the song.

American record producers sensed a hot publicity item
and rushed to put a translated version on the market. Sam
M. Lewis (who also wrote such favorites as "Five Foot Two,
Eyes of Blue," "Dinah," "I'm Sitting on Top of the World,"
and "Absence Makes the Heart Grow Fonder") came up with
the English lyrics, and by March 1936 the American public
could choose from three recorded versions—from bandleaders
Paul Whiteman, Hal Kemp, and Henry King. With question-
able delicacy, "Gloomy Sunday" was heavily promoted as
"The Famous Hungarian Suicide Song."

The song *is* a sad one. It tells the story of a mourner
whose lover has just died ("Angels have no thought of ever
returning you."), and who contemplates ending it all for the
hope of reunion ("Would they be angry if I thought of joining
you?"). But apparently Lewis's translation did not have the
power of the original Hungarian. The song grew quite pop-

15

ular on the legend of its death-inducing properties—Artie Shaw, Vincent Lopez, Paul Robeson, and Billie Holliday all recorded it—but American audiences seemed able to resist its dark message. No "Gloomy Sunday" suicides were reported, and radio stations played the song without restriction.

"Gloomy Sunday" brought wealth to its Hungarian composer, but not happiness. In 1968, at the age of 69, Reszo Seress committed suicide by leaping from a Budapest building.

===

★ ★ The flu epidemic that followed World War I was caused by poisoned gases that circled the globe like invisible tornados. (1918)

Not true. The epidemic was the most widespread and deadly in modern times, and, because it began during the war, it stirred up much suspicious but uninformed talk. The virus is believed to have stricken 200 million people—roughly a tenth of the human race at the time—and to have caused 20 million deaths worldwide. It felled half as many soldiers worldwide as died in battle in France.

The disease first took hold in Madrid in May 1918, swiftly spreading through Spain and the rest of Europe, then finally gaining a foothold in the United States at the end of the summer, carried by soldiers returning from the war. Wild stories of its origin first appeared in Spain, where people blamed the disease on the Germans. The strongest theory was that the German troops, weakened by hunger and lack of proper clothing, had bred the disease and that the bacteria had come to Spain in the strong coastal winds during the winter. Others thought the disease had been deliberately planted in Spain by the infected crews of German submarines. Neither theory accounted for the fact that the first flu outbreak occurred in the inland city of Madrid, but, as the disease spread, so did both the rumors.

★ ★ An American prisoner of war in a Japanese prison camp wrote home to his family that he was being treated well by his captors. He ended the letter by asking his mother to save the stamp on the envelope for his collection. The mother soaked the stamp off and found written beneath it, "They have cut out my tongue." (1942)

Not true. This horror rumor surfaced in a number of guises during the Civil War, World War I, and World War II. Sometimes it is called the "Little Alf" story, because in one version the prisoner allegedly ended his letter with the words, "save the stamp for little Alf." His mother became suspicious; it seems she didn't know anyone named little Alf. A key fact that undermined this story in all its versions is that prisoners of war's letters aren't (and never have been) stamped by the prisoners.

Swarms of rumors made the rounds during World War II, many of them having to do with waste and betrayal within our own forces or on the part of our allies. The Navy was said to have dumped three carloads of coffee into New York harbor. The Army was throwing away whole sides of beef.

17

Most of the butter produced in the U.S. was being shipped to Russia, where it was used for greasing guns. The Red Cross was charging American soldiers in Iceland outrageous prices for sweaters knit by volunteers in the United States. Black women were using Eleanor Clubs, sponsored by Eleanor Roosevelt, as a cover for an organization bent on fomenting general rebellion—they were supposedly collecting guns and icepicks for the violent day, and their alleged motto was "Every white woman in her own kitchen in a year!" The tallest of the Watts Towers—Simon Rodia's hand-built steel towers in Los Angeles—was being used as a Japanese radio transmitter, broadcasting the voice of Tokyo Rose, rumored to be a native of Watts herself. After the attack on Pearl Harbor on December 7, 1941, stories were told in Hawaii that local Japanese workers had cut arrows in the cane fields as guides for the attacking bombers; that a Honolulu high school ring had been found on the body of one of the downed Japanese fliers; and that local Japanese had been forewarned of the attack by an advertisement in a Honolulu newspaper on December 6. Perhaps the most ridiculous story of all circulated in the Northwest in 1942—that Japanese saboteurs, disguised as salmon, were swimming up the Columbia River. One of them was rumored to have been captured by Federal agents. (We wonder what sort of lure they used.)

In an effort to combat these clearly divisive stories, several rumor clinics were set up around the country to provide a forum for exposing and refuting the false assertions. Newspapers and magazines ran regular "rumor columns" during the war to try to stop the stories from spreading. We will never know if the clinics or the columns stemmed the growth of any of the rumors, but they did do us a service by collecting and documenting the stories.

★ ★ A tidal wave swallowed New York City at the same time the earthquake hit San Francisco. (immediately after the 1906 earthquake)

Filippo Giansanti

Not true. Other rumors rampant right after the disaster were that Chicago had dropped into Lake Michigan, that the earthquake had loosed the animals from their cages in the San Francisco Zoo and that they were eating the refugees from the disaster who had fled to Golden Gate Park, and that looters had been found with women's fingers in their pockets (they had allegedly been in too much of a hurry to take the rings off).

These rumors sprang up largely because normal news sources had been cut off, and people were desperate for information. Such welters of rumor often occur in disaster situations or in wartime—whenever the public wants more news than it can get from the established news media. After the great Indian earthquake of January 15, 1934, strange rumors flooded the disaster area—that the river Ganges had vanished, along with all the bathers who had been in it; that not one person was left alive in North Bihar; that astrologers had correctly predicted the earthquake and that they now predicted a terrible day on January 23 and gender changes for all on February 27. (Both these rumored days of apocalypse came and went without incident.)

★ ★ The tiny letters "JS" on the Roosevelt dime stand for "Joseph Stalin." (1948)

Not true. They are the initials of the designer of the coin, John Sinnock. A similar story claims that a small hammer and sickle can be found on the Kennedy half dollar, at the base of Kennedy's neck. This mark is actually the stylized initials of Gilroy Roberts, who designed that side of the coin. Neither rumor makes clear how the subversive marks were supposed to have made their way onto the coins. Were they the work of enemy agents within our own treasury department? And what effect were the marks supposed to have on us?

Rumors also surround a set of mysterious numbers on the five dollar bill—they are found in the bushes to the left of the Lincoln Memorial steps. Some see a "372," some a "3179." Are they a telephone number? An address? A room number? The rumors claim so, but the Treasury Department dismisses the digits as an accident.

Irish nationalists were blamed for a rumored defacement of Canadian currency issued in 1954. Supposedly a devil's face had been slyly etched into Queen Elizabeth's hair and was printed in all denominations. This story was published as fact in a 1982 issue of *Parade* magazine, which revived the rumor after thirty years. A close examination of the actual bill shows that the public's vivid imagination was the moving force behind the "devil's face"—not any Irish nationalists.

★ ★ George Washington was the father of our country in more ways than one. His romantic exploits led to the births of several illegitimate children. (1790s)

Not true. As our country's first president, Washington became the first to feel the sting of the rumors that have since plagued American politicians. In Britain, where the voters elect representatives to Parliament who then choose a prime minister, a politician's position on the issues is the primary factor in his consideration for highest office. In the United States, where voters more directly elect one person to head the government, personality often supplants the issues as the dominant factor in a campaign. If a politician can get no results by attacking a foe on the issues, he sometimes stoops to an attack on his opponent's personality. Rumors have served this devious purpose in campaign after campaign.

Four separate slanderous attacks were made on Washington during his illustrious career. The first concerned a letter he allegedly sent a friend, inviting him to Mt. Vernon and mentioning the attractions of a certain slave girl as an inducement. The letter has never been brought to light, and the witnesses who claimed to have seen it always turned out to be of the third hand sort so common in rumors. A second rumor claimed that Washington had kept up an affair with a New Jersey woman named Mary Gibbons while he head-quartered in New York during the Revolution. According to this rumor, Washington regularly rowed across the Hudson River at night to visit her. The stories sometimes went a step further to allege that Miss Gibbons had been a British spy and had received important information from Washington during their trysts. That the story was first promoted in a Tory pamphlet is indication enough of its falsity. Another rumor connected Washington with an illegitimate son who became a well-known officer in the Continental Army. According to this tale, Washington was only eighteen when he fathered the boy, and he made good his mistake by paying for the child's education. Washington actually did fund the educations of several young men, but if he was the father of all of them he must have been a busy ladies' man. Another rumor about Washington's immoral relations with his slaves was started by an angry army officer, Major General Charles Lee, after his court-martial for unnecessary retreat in battle. In his humiliation, Lee managed to strike a real blow at General Washington, for the rumor stuck. With added embellishments—such as the assertion that numerous children survived to prove the story—the rumor persisted, and it is still in circulation after nearly two hundred years.

When Washington assumed the presidency, he wrote a friend, "My movements to the chair of government will be accompanied by feelings not unlike those of a culprit who is going to his place of execution." His decision not to run for a third term was influenced in great part by the attacks on his character. The rumor mill even churned out a final story after Washington's death—that he had succumbed to pneumonia caught while visiting a lady friend on a snowy night. At least he never had to hear that one.

A popular adage holds that in England the open possession of a mistress would badly damage the career of a politician, while in France it would make no difference, and in Italy it might give a candidate the winning edge. In the United States it would certainly ruin him. Thomas Jefferson's campaign was hurt by rumors that he had fathered several children by one of his slaves, Sally Henning, and that he had deflowered the daughter of a prominent Virginia gentleman while a guest at her parents' home. The first story seems to be gaining historical credence, though all the evidence so far uncovered is decidedly circumstantial. The second rumor has been shown to be a malicious fabrication. In spite of those whispers, and another that held that he was a drunkard and an atheist who planned to burn bibles, Jefferson won the election.

When Andrew Jackson and John Quincy Adams campaigned against each other in 1828, both were plagued by rumors of immoral conduct. Adams was said to have sold an American girl into white slavery while serving as U.S. minister in Russia. Jackson was charged with living in sin with his wife for two years before marrying her. In fact the couple *had* lived together improperly, though it was by an honest accident: Mrs. Jackson thought a divorce from her previous husband had been granted, when in fact it had not. As soon as the Jacksons discovered their mistake, the divorce was finalized and they remarried. Jackson won the election in spite of the rumors. All through the campaign he had protected his wife from the slander, but he couldn't keep it from her forever. She finally read the story in a Washington newspaper, and it affected her so strongly that her health completely failed. She died within three weeks.

Some other rumors of sexual misconduct turned out to have a grain of truth behind them. In 1884 Grover Cleveland admitted to having fathered an illegitimate son in his youth. His honesty, and the fact that he had always provided for the woman and child to the best of his ability, defused what could have been a damaging rumor. Still, antagonistic crowds often jeered him with the chant, "Ma, Ma, where's my pa? Gone to the White House. Ha! Ha! Ha!" The stories about Warren Harding's various misconducts—especially of his keeping of a young mistress while in office—almost certainly had a foundation in truth. Nan Britton's kiss-and-tell bestseller, which came out after Harding's death, is probably not a complete fabrication. The circumstances of his death have never been fully revealed, and rumors continue to surround it—claiming that he was poisoned by his wife, or that he suffered a heart attack while engaged in sex with a mistress.

Tales of John F. Kennedy's romantic exploits could fill a small book. One strange and entirely false story told during his 1960 campaign asserted that Jacqueline Bouvier was his second wife—that he had earlier married and divorced another woman.

Improper parentage has served as a close rival to immoral conduct as a source of scandalous political rumor. When Andrew Jackson ran for reelection in 1832, he no longer had a wife, so the rumors focused on his birth. According to a fabricated report in the Cincinnati *Gazette,* "General Jackson's mother was a common prostitute, brought to this country by British soldiers. She afterward married a MULATTO MAN with whom she had several children, of whom General Jackson is one." Similar rumors have attached themselves to other candidates. Martin Van Buren was whispered to be the illegitimate son of Aaron Burr. Even Abraham Lincoln was rumored to be a bastard, the illegitimate son of—variously—Henry Clay, John C. Calhoun, Abraham Inlow, Andrew Marshall, and a handful of other notables.

Other candidates have been the subject of whispers about their use of alcohol and drugs. If these stories are to be believed, our country has been in the unsteady control of drunkards more often than not. The list includes John

Adams, Thomas Jefferson, Martin Van Buren, William Henry Harrison, James Polk, Abraham Lincoln, Andrew Johnson, Grover Cleveland, Benjamin Harrison, Theodore Roosevelt, Warren G. Harding, Franklin D. Roosevelt, and John F. Kennedy.

The one reassuring aspect of this litany of slanderous political rumors is that the stories have so rarely brought defeat to their targets.

★ ★ Mount Rainier, in Washington, was given its name in order to promote the sale of Rainier beer. (1930s)

Not true. This rumor roused the fury of the people of Tacoma to such an extent that the issue was brought to the floor of Congress—where it was finally dropped without action. According to the rumor, the brewery shipped a carload of its Rainier beer to the Washington board that was naming the mountain, thus persuading them not to choose the name that local residents favored: Mount Tacoma. In fact, the mountain was named in 1792 by Captain George Vancouver, the British explorer. The settlers of Tacoma did try for years to have the name changed to Mount Tacoma, but their requests were denied. The matter was settled long before the brewery started bubbling.

★ ★ While in office President Grover Cleveland underwent a secret operation for the removal of his upper jaw. (1893)

True. The remarkable thing about this rumor is that it turned out to be so accurate, though it was based on what seemed at the time to be wild speculation. The president did indeed undergo a major operation for the removal of a cancerous growth in his upper jaw, and, for political reasons, the operation was kept a closely guarded secret. The full details of the president's activities during the summer of 1893 were not made public for almost twenty-five years, until in 1917 one of the surgeons finally revealed the truth.

On June 18, 1893, Dr. R. M. Reilly was asked to examine a slight roughness on the roof of the president's mouth and discovered an ulcer the size of a quarter. This turned out to be a dangerous malignant growth. On June 30, the president abruptly left Washington for what was announced as a month's vacation at his home, Gray Gables, on Buzzard's Bay in Massachusetts. He traveled by train to New York, where he boarded a friend's yacht for the second leg of the voyage.

That night, as the yacht slowly steamed up the East River, a team of four doctors and a dentist removed Cleveland's entire upper left jaw. On July 5, the boat arrived in Buzzard's Bay, where the president was able to walk from the dock to his house. While he recuperated from the operation, an artificial jaw was fashioned from vulcanized rubber. The president traveled to Washington briefly on August 7 for the opening of the special session of Congress—though after four days he returned to Gray Gables for another month of recuperation.

During August and September rumors about the operation and the president's ill health circulated widely, making their way onto the pages of some less principled newspapers. All these stories were vigorously denied, though in fact they were entirely accurate. Cleveland finally silenced the talk when he gave a rousing speech on September 18 commemorating the anniversary of the construction of the Capitol. Scores of reporters were on hand, looking for any clue of an operation, but they found none—a tribute to the good fit of the vulcanized rubber jaw. The *New York Times* reported that the president was "a man in the flush of vigorous health, clear eyed, strong . . . and when he spoke his voice rang out over the crowd so that it could be heard by the furthermost listener." He lived for fifteen more years.

★ ★ The Smithsonian Institution in Washington D.C. has in its collection the pickled penis of gangster John Dillinger. It was preserved because of its extraordinary size. (1940s)

Not true. Because of the Smithsonian Institution's vast and wide-ranging holdings—from colonial documents to turn-of-the-century food packages to props from television programs—a number of rumors have cropped up over the years wrongly attributing some incredible items to the collection. Just where did believers think the museum was going to display the Dillinger specimen, we wonder? With the weapons of other notorious outlaws? The rumor probably got its start in the confusion that followed Dillinger's death in 1934. (For rumors of his survival, see page 115.) The "coroner" who accepted the body at the Cook County Morgue was actually

28

a reporter for the *Chicago Tribune*. During the course of the inquest and autopsy Dillinger's brain was removed and somehow mislaid. It was never recovered, and it is probably this mishap that planted the seed of the Smithsonian rumor. One ambitious businessman offered the outlaw's father $10,000 for the body, but was turned down. Mr. Dillinger did announce that he would consider "propositions for other things John had." We're almost certain that by "other things" he did not mean parts of his son's body.

Another artifact wrongly rumored to be stored in the Smithsonian's vaults is the skull of Sitting Bull, the Sioux chieftain who led his warriors to victory against General Custer. Curators at the Smithsonian have been denying this one for years. Sitting Bull is actually buried whole at Fort Yates, North Dakota.

In the forties many people believed that the Smithsonian had the stuffed remains of one of the country's most remarkable cats. According to the story, the durable tabby survived a fall from the top of the Washington Monument only to be killed by a dog as it tried to run away.

A museum in Paris, the Musée de l'Homme, counts some famous human specimens among its eerie inventory. The museum—something of a relic itself—was founded in the nineteenth century by the great French anatomist and anthropologist Paul Broca as a center for the study of human anatomy. As part of his legacy to the collection, he left it his own brain. It now floats in a jar on the museum's shelves, surrounded by such notable specimens as the skull of Descartes and the preserved genitalia of the Hottentot Venus— a once-famous carnival performer. A fascinating account of the museum can be found in Carl Sagan's book *Broca's Brain*.

★ ★ Mary Baker Eddy, the founder of the Christian Science Church, was buried with a telephone in case she ever needed to make a call from the other side. (1910)

Not true. The construction of Eddy's white marble tomb at Mount Auburn Cemetery in Cambridge, Massachusetts, was so involved that a telephone was installed at the site to keep the workers in close touch with their home office. This apparently sparked the rumor, though the phone was taken out as soon as the memorial was finished. Workers at Mount Auburn say they still get plenty of questions about

Eddy's phone—more than seventy years after her death.

The same rumor is associated with Aimee Semple McPherson, the flamboyant radio evangelist, who was buried in 1944 in Los Angeles's Forest Lawn Memorial Park. McPherson used a telephone on the stage of her Angelus Temple to keep in contact with her radio crew during sermons, and this may have led to the rumor. More likely, people just confused her with Mary Baker Eddy.

★ ★ Orange Fiesta Ware is radioactive. (1940s)

Partly true. Fiesta Ware, a line of brightly colored dishes first produced in 1936 by the Homer-Laughlin China Company, originally came in five colors, one of them a vivid orange. The color was taken off the market in the forties, and a rumor spread that the orange dishes were radioactive.

In 1981 that rumor was substantiated when the New York State Department of Health warned against eating regularly from the orange dishes because the glaze contains lead and uranium compounds, both of which tend to be absorbed by acidic foods. Ingested lead may, over a long period of time, cause stomach disorders and worse, and ingested uranium may cause kidney dysfunction. The uranium also emits low levels of radiation. However, it is not dangerous to use the dishes as decorative objects.

Rumors about radioactivity are widespread, and, in many cases, they turn out to be based on real dangers. In the twenties, many women subjected themselves to X-ray hair-removal treatments, and a frightening percentage later suffered from skin cancer. Stories about radiation perils again made the rounds in the forties, when X-ray shoe-fitting devices became common fixtures in shoe stores, largely as an attraction for children. Some of these machines gave off huge amounts of radiation, and children were often allowed to play with them for long stretches of time. Besides causing a higher risk of cancer, excessive X-ray exposure posed a real threat to the growth tissue in children's bones. One young professional shoe model was so severely burned with radiation from a fitting device that part of one foot had to be amputated. Before the 1963 Nuclear Test Ban Treaty, in the days when atomic bombs were exploded in the open atmosphere, it really was dangerous at times to eat snow and drink rainwater—and we thought that was just a rumor.

But, lest you believe *everything* you hear about radiation, some radioactive rumors are just bunk. After the accident at the Three-Mile Island nuclear power plant in 1979, a story spread that Hershey's chocolate—made near the damaged plant—had been irradiated. It just wasn't so, as high government officials quickly pointed out. A statement was issued from the White House that "the food from the Three-Mile Island area is as safe to produce, buy, transport, prepare, and eat as the food available at any other place in the U.S." Fortunately for Hershey's, the rumor fizzled rapidly, and sales weren't greatly affected. (Incidentally, the main street in Hershey, Pennsylvania really *is* lined with street lights shaped like Hershey's Kisses.)

━━

★ ★ Exiled Argentine dictator Juan Peron keeps the embalmed body of Eva Peron, dead for twenty years, in his Madrid home, where he props her up in a chair to join him for dinner. (1971)

Not true. While Eva Peron lived as first lady of Argentina, wife of president Juan Peron from 1946 until her death in 1952, she was held in almost saintlike regard by much of the country. Born poor herself, she championed the cause of the poor and the working class, and successfully campaigned for women's suffrage. She died of cancer at the age of thirty-three, and her body was carefully embalmed over a period of six months by Dr. Pedro Ara, a Spanish pathologist. When Juan Peron was overthrown in 1955, Eva's elaborate tomb remained unfinished, and her body fell into the hands of the anti-Peronist leaders. For the next fifteen years the government of Argentina kept the corpse hidden, at first in a packing case marked "radio sets" in a warehouse in Buenos Aires, then in a storeroom at the Argentine embassy in Bonn, and finally in a grave marked "Maggi" in Milan. The lengths they went to to hide the body attest to Eva Peron's political power, even in death.

In 1971, responding to a change in political climate, a new government disentombed the body and made a gift of it to Juan Peron, then living in exile in Madrid. When the body arrived, the same Dr. Ara who had embalmed her helped Peron and his new wife Isabel unpack her. Much to the doctor's pride, Eva was in nearly perfect condition. According to his memoirs, one ear was bent, a fingertip was broken off, and some cracks had appeared in the plastic coating, but he had clearly done his job well. The body remained with the Perons in Madrid for just over a year, and it was this cohabitation that started the macabre rumor.

Peron returned to power in Argentina at the end of 1972, though he lived for only another year and a half. When he died, his body too was embalmed, and Eva was flown from Madrid to lie in state at his side. Since then forces unfriendly to Peron have again come to power, and, though Eva's body has been buried in an officially marked crypt, some Argentinians again wonder where she is, whether she has again been secretly moved, and whether the body brought from Madrid after twenty years was really hers or was just a wax dummy.

★ ★ Teflon, DuPont's non-stick coating for frying pans, gives off poisonous fumes when heated. (1955)

Not true. Teflon is a perfectly safe material for cooking, as it is for its myriad of other uses.* The first versions of the rumor told of a machinist who died after smoking a cigarette contaminated with a small amount of Teflon resin. In the most dramatic versions, he took one puff on the cigarette, his lungs filled up with fluid, and he died within five minutes. The story, though entirely false, spread widely, helped along by occasional appearances in military and industrial safety bulletins.

DuPont may have unwittingly planted the seed of the rumor when the product was first introduced. The company warned early users that mild and temporary toxic effects might be produced by Teflon under conditions of extreme heat and poor ventilation. DuPont later had cause to regret that warning when it discovered a market for the plastic as a lining for greaseless frying pans.

The non-stick pans were first introduced in Europe, where three French laboratories conducted independent studies and found the rumors groundless. Meanwhile, DuPont's diligent patroling of American industrial and military publications had yielded printed retractions of the false stories. The inspector general of the Air Force judged the rumor

---

*One of the most fascinating of Teflon's applications can be seen at the Forest Lawn Memorial Park in Glendale, California, where a huge marble replica of Michelangelo's David rests on a layer of Teflon as protection from earthquake damage. If all goes according to plan, the statue will slip and slide in place during the next big earthquake and not shatter, as did its pre-Teflon predecessor.

"completely unsubstantiated." By 1960, DuPont felt that the rumor was finally dead and decided it was at last safe to sell America the Teflon pan. But, even as the pans were shipped to stores, the rumor resurfaced with a vengeance, easily outpacing DuPont's rumor patrol.

Here is an example of how the story traveled through safety publications: In May 1961, an Air Force installation in Texas ran the rumor in a bulletin. After a call from DuPont, a retraction was printed the next month, but not before an Air Force publication in Michigan picked up the original falsehood. The Michigan story was read at a fire chief's convention in Detroit and jumped from there to a report from the British Columbia Fire Chief's Association. A doctor read the story there and relayed the news in a letter to a journal of the Canadian Medical Association.

The damaging falsehood seemed to slip through DuPont's safety net at every turn. The company got retractions every time the story appeared in print, but the growing edge of the rumor always seemed just out of reach. For a time in 1962, DuPont executives considered pulling the Teflon pans off the market until the rumor subsided.

Luckily they didn't have to make that move. Enough pans got into kitchens around the country where enough cooks fried food in them without ill effect that the rumor was quashed by demonstration. Little was heard of the story after 1963.

★ ★ The fluid at the center of a golf ball is a powerful explosive. (1950s)

Not true. Countless children have spent countless hours disemboweling liquid-center golf balls for the thrill of unraveling yards of elastic and finding at the center the mysterious dark little ball filled with who-knows-what. The rumor usually has it that the liquid is an acid sure to blind whoever tampers with it, but in some gentler versions of the story it's claimed that the substance is honey or Karo syrup. The spokesperson for one large golf-ball manufacturer told us that his company uses water in the center of its golf balls; a different company told us that it used a mild oil; and another told us that it filled the center of its balls with a solution of water and salts that could be irritating to the eyes. Some early golf balls had glycerine or paste in their centers, but no golf-ball maker has ever filled its balls with an explosive substance. People persist in believing this, however, and the receptionist at one company told us that she has fielded many inquiries from pet owners fearful that their dogs were about to self-destruct from eating golf balls.

Several manufacturers pointed out to us that the elastic thread inside a liquid-center golf ball is wound so tightly that if the ball is damaged it could "pop" from the force of the elastic spinning off, but it would never *explode*. One plucky company representative told us that when he once sliced the interior ball to see what would happen, it too just "popped" and a bit of liquid spurted out.

Nevertheless, if you do get some golf-ball fluid in your eyes or know of a child or pet who ingests some, to be on the safe side, call the maker of the specific ball and ask for the lowdown on its liquid center. Chances are that it's harmless, but if the ball is one of the few varieties that contains a solution of "salts," your doctor will want to know about it.

★ ★ If you send a 1943 copper penny to the Ford Motor Company, they will send you a new Ford car. (1947)

Not true. Although this one turns out to have a strange twist. In 1943, in an effort to conserve copper for the war effort, the U.S. Mint made pennies out of steel with a zinc plating. So the rumor about the 1943 copper penny seems at first to be a sort of joke—there aren't any 1943 copper pennies. But it turns out that there *are*. And they are extremely rare. Only eleven have been found as of this writing, the most recent one discovered in 1975. They were minted by mistake and unwittingly put into circulation, where it is conceivable that one or two may still be found. And here's the best part: the last one sold, in 1978, went for $4,300— just about enough to buy a new Ford car that year. But let us add a word of caution. Anything so simple and so valuable is an easy target for fakery, and there are roughly fifty thousand copper-*plated* 1943 pennies—deliberate frauds with ordinary steel centers—waiting out there to fool you. So before you trade your car for a penny, have the coin examined by a reputable coin dealer.

For some reason the Ford Company attracted an undue number of wishful rumors, perhaps because people thought of Henry Ford as a fabulously wealthy businessman who was sympathetic to those who had to struggle for a living. In 1924, Mr. Ford received over 500 thousand personal letters asking for money and free cars, some from people responding to local rumors of his generosity, others from dreamers with fantastic schemes. Many people seemed to believe that he would give a free car to anyone who enclosed return postage in a letter. People who wrote with that request often explained that a friend or neighbor had assured them it was so. One woman proposed a deal that would land her needed cash without costing Mr. Ford a cent. All he had to do was lend her $1,000, invest it for her until it had appreciated in value to $100,000, then repay himself and send her the $99,000 in earnings. Ford employed an office of secretaries to set these people straight.

Two other coin-for-a-car myths were undoubtedly based on this mistaken perception of Ford as a source of handouts. A 1918 rumor held that the company had secretly put four specially marked dimes in circulation—each stamped with a letter from the word "Ford" in the place of the mint identification—and that the four lucky finders would get brand new Ford cars. A lot of people wasted time counting change extra carefully that year.

A few years later the legend surfaced in another form— that Ford would give a free car to anyone who brought in a dime minted in 1922. This time the rumormongers were dreaming. No dimes were minted in 1922, nor were any nickels, quarters, or half dollars.

The "something for nothing" rumors occupy an enduring place in our culture. They reaffirm our belief that anyone can make it big with a little luck—that easy street can be just around the corner. And the stories aren't really so far-fetched. In 1980 a box of Crackerjacks went on the market with a coupon inside redeemable for a new car. An art professor won two successive million-dollar lotteries in 1977, then retired from teaching to pursue his art full time. Think of the lotteries and contests you yourself have entered. And don't try to tell us you won't have an eye out for that 1943 copper penny. Finding that coin is an American dream.

★ ★ Rolls Royce engines are sealed at the factory so that no one but a Rolls Royce mechanic can work on them. (Since 1904)

Not true. The company denies this. Besides, as a spokesperson for Rolls Royce Motors has pointed out, how could anyone change the oil if the engine were sealed? However, it *is* true that the underside of every Rolls Royce is studded with sixty-four nuts that are painted yellow at the factory so that a Rolls-Royce-trained eye can tell if anyone else has worked on the car.

The Rolls Royce seems to have captured more rumor-prone imaginations than any other car. Another rumor that has persisted for decades is that the Rolls Royce warranty provides that the company will send a mechanic anywhere in the world to work on the car if it breaks down (or, as the company puts it, "if it fails to proceed"). This isn't true, either, but the company does have seventy dealers and six zone offices in the United States, each equipped with a mechanic who has been specially trained to work on Rolls Royces. The

Rolls rumor also exists in a more elaborate version, complete with exotic locale and surprise ending. It goes like this: a touring party was stranded in the south of France when its Rolls Royce "failed to proceed." The owner called Rolls Royce in England, and soon a group of mechanics materialized to replace the half-shaft. When the grateful owner later called to ask what the charge would be, he was told that the company had no record of the incident.

In the thirties rumor had it that the company had changed the badge on the front of the radiator from red to black to commemorate the death of Henry Royce in 1933. The truth is that the color of the badge did change in 1933, but because Henry Royce thought that black fit with the color scheme of the car better than red, and it was pure coincidence that the change went into effect in the year of his death.

Rumor also has it that the statuette on the front of the car, called the "Spirit of Ecstasy," was modeled on the figure of Eleanor Thornton, the mistress of a well-known British aristocrat. This one *is* true. Charles Rolls, who died in a flying accident in 1910 at the age of thirty-three, never had the pleasure of meeting the sylph, who first appeared on Rolls Royces in 1911. She did make the acquaintance of Stalin, Lenin, Mao Tse Tung, and Lawrence of Arabia, all of whom owned Rolls Royces.

★ ★ You can buy World War II-vintage Harley-Davidson motorcycles from the U.S. government for fifty dollars. They come unassembled with the parts packed in grease. (1950s)

Not true. The Harley-Davidson Motor Company speculates that this rumor got its start right after World War II when a limited number of motorcycles were sold for low prices as government surplus. But no such great deal has been offered since then, which is too bad, because a World War II-vintage Harley-Davidson in mint condition is one of the most desirable motorized collectibles around.

Sometimes this rumor is told with a "catch" at the end: that the motorcycles are only available in lots of fifty—a cruel twist that has probably left countless teenagers crestfallen.

A related rumor has it that World War II-vintage jeeps, also unassembled and packed in grease, can be had from the government for the same low price of fifty dollars. This rumor is also not true.

★ ★ Some gamblers are so good at blackjack that they are barred from casinos around the world. (1960s)

Partly true. The most sophisticated blackjack players rely on a system of "counting," that can, when combined with other playing strategies, shift the balance of chance to their favor.

The object of blackjack—or twenty-one—is for the players and the dealer to approach as nearly as possible a card count of twenty-one without going higher (called "breaking"). Numbered cards are counted at their value, face cards at ten, and aces at either one or eleven. The most direct way of reaching twenty-one is to draw an ace (worth eleven) and a face card (worth ten). By Nevada rules, up to seven players bet against the dealer, whose play is automatic—he must draw another card on a sixteen or lower, and stand pat on a seventeen or higher.

The strategy for players involves the amount of their bets and the decision of whether to stand pat or to draw another card. The key to any winning system is to learn which cards are left in the deck to be dealt and to bet on this knowledge to one's advantage. Players learn what is in the deck by "counting" the cards played. They take advantage of their knowledge by betting heavily when the cards left in the deck are distributed in their favor.

Casinos watch for counters, and, when they spot one winning large amounts of money, they frequently bar him (or her) from the game. The better blackjack players naturally resent this, but lawsuits brought by them to stop the practice have so far ended in favor of the casinos. Players sometimes escape the notice of the casino bouncer by playing in teams and signalling to each other so that it always looks as though a newcomer to the game has made a lucky win, while in reality a player familiar with the deal from the deck has picked the opportune moment for the bet.

Very few players are both adept enough to count in the fast-paced game and cool enough as gamblers to turn the system to their advantage. Even many of the "experts" who have written books and articles about winning systems find that they actually lose as much money as the unindoctrinated novice—often more, because of their stubborn faith in the method. But the myth of blackjack as a game that can be beat serves as one of gambling's biggest drawing cards. The counters do the casinos a favor by luring countless losers to the twenty-one tables.

★ ★ The Seeing Eye Foundation will provide a free seeing-eye dog to a needy blind person for every collection of twenty-five thousand empty matchbook covers brought in to them. (1940s)

Not true. This rumor began in Philadelphia and spread across the country, evolving along the way to apply to empty cigarette packages, quantities of tin foil, and even string. The version we first heard, in the late fifties, called for miles of gum-wrapper chains—the kind you make by folding up the paper wrapping. We fell for it like everyone else. It gave us a sense of mission as we spent hour after wasted hour folding wrappers into longer and longer chains. When we thought we had enough links, we checked back with our source of information and realized with horror that nobody knew where to send them. Talk about wasted energy—we could have been watching television! Unfortunately the rumor can be much more emotionally devastating to the people who are expecting to receive the seeing-eye dogs.

Not all such collection stories are rumors. The Campbell Soup Company is currently sponsoring a "Labels for Education" program in a few selected test cities. Under special conditions, quantities of soup-can labels can be redeemed by schools for sports equipment. Schools and churches sometimes sponsor coupon drives to obtain food and gifts for the poor.

And, lest you think that clipping coupons is a matter of nickels and dimes, a woman in Philadelphia brought a car dealer to court in December 1982 for failing to live up to his coupon offer. She collected thirty-nine of his "$100-off" newspaper coupons from friends and relatives, and brought them in, demanding to collect her car. It seems that the dealer hadn't limited the offer to one coupon per customer.

★ ★ If you can peel the label from a bottle of beer in one piece with your fingernail you are a virgin. (1950s)

Who knows? These virgin-indicator rumors have taken a number of different forms. Some pre-teenagers swear that you are truly chaste only if you can peel the foil from a chewing-gum wrapper in one piece, or if the cartilage at the end of your nose feels like it's in two pieces. In the early sixties rumor had it that you could tell a lot about a girl by where she wore her circle pin. If she wore it on the left side of her sweater, she was a virgin—or was it on the right side of her sweater? No one could ever quite remember which side meant what. One false move and you were in instant disrepute.

Rumor also has it that the lions in front of the New York Public Library will roar when a virgin walks by, but they apparently haven't spotted one yet.

★ ★ If you grow your fingernails over an inch long and send them to Revlon, they will send you ten dollars. (1960s)

Not true. But that hasn't stopped a lot of ambitious types from trying. Revlon still has trouble with this rumor, according to the long-suffering head of the consumer relations department. Mothers call, worried because their daughters are starting to look like Balinese dancers, and the nail-growers themselves often call to check on the rates before they send in their clippings. Most are adamant in their refusal to believe the news that the company doesn't buy nails. Some complain that a good friend just sold *her* nails *last week*, or that someone they know got the reward by showing up in person and cutting her nails right in the Revlon offices. The consumer relations staff has become accustomed over the years to fielding these calls, and to opening letters from customers and watching ultra-long fingernails drop out.

The rumor has apparently kept pace with inflation—some of the nail-growers now want as much as one hundred dollars for a thumbnail, and only slightly less for the nails of other fingers.

Revlon's reply to the claimants is considerate but blunt: "There has never been any truth to the rumor that we buy fingernails. Thank you for checking directly with us nonetheless. We congratulate you on your healthy nails and hope you will let Revlon help you keep them long and attractive."

★ ★ Howard Hughes, the famous and reclusive billionaire, let his hair and fingernails grow very long during his last years of life. (1960s)

True. According to Bob Roberts, one of Hughes's personal detectives, he let his hair grow to the middle of his back and his fingernails and toenails to a length of five or six inches. Maybe Hughes had heard the Revlon story and was planning to make a killing in nail futures. We'll never know for sure what motives he had for his often peculiar behavior, as he maintained a dense cloud of secrecy around himself. Rumors about his last years in Las Vegas maintained that Hughes had swung the other way—that he had cleaned himself up; that he had been spotted in London getting a haircut; that he had taken up flying again and was making a trip around the world. Some stories held that it was not Hughes at all, but a double sitting in the tiny room atop the Desert Inn in Las Vegas. We do know that Hughes died in 1972 aboard a plane flying to Texas from Mexico—the fingerprints were checked. But the autopsy results are cloaked in secrecy.

★ ★ The tiny stars on the cover of *Playboy,* printed inside or next to the letter "P," are a code to show whether Hugh Hefner slept with the featured Playmate of the Month. (1960s)

Not true. According to the rumor, Hugh Hefner announced his sexual triumphs to his readers each month in a not-so-secret code, to be found in the number of little stars on the cover of *Playboy.* Some thought that the stars were Hugh's rating system, telling the world how "good" the model had been in bed. Others thought the stars showed how many times the two had had sex—covers were sometimes found with as many as six stars, apparently Hefner's personal record.

The stories made for titillating fantasies, and *Playboy* never went out of its way to deny them. But when asked, they have always admitted that the stars have a much more mundane message. *Playboy* comes out in six different advertising editions—one for the military and five for different regions of the country—each of which contains the same editorial pages, but a different set of ads, targeted to the different editions' audiences. The stars are a code used to mark the editions and were used mainly by the shipping center to see that the various editions went where they were supposed to go.

A more efficient production system allowed *Playboy* to abandon the star code in 1979. We imagine that there are still some readers out there who think that Hugh Hefner suddenly lost his virility that year.

A variation of the rumor found the key to the code in the placement of the stars. If they were inside the letter "P," Hugh had "gotten lucky" that month. If they were outside the letter, he'd been spurned. In fact, since the stars were always printed in black, they were simply placed against the lightest background for visibility. If a dark color was chosen for the word "Playboy," the stars appeared just outside the letter "P"; they showed up inside the letter if the title printed in a lighter color.

★ ★ A woman got what she thought was the perfect beehive hairdo at the hairdresser's, and she was so pleased with it that she left it in for days, spraying more and more hairspray on it and never washing it. She ended up at a hospital with a terrific pain on the top of her head, and when they took apart the hairdo the doctors found that a black widow spider had moved in and had bitten her on the head. The woman died soon afterward. (1950s)

Not true. This story, and it is really more of a story than a rumor, is usually introduced as having actually happened to a friend of a friend of a friend, or "someone my mother's best friend knows." It was widely told in the sixties and is still making the rounds, though the beehive hairdo is now changed to a "hairdresser do," or the story is related as a memory from high school. It is clearly told as a sort of cautionary tale—with the moral being to wash your hair regularly, or to beware of silly and extravagant fashions.

A variant told in the late sixties had a hippie as the slovenly one. He never washed his hair, and finally a spider bit him on the head or a mouse burrowed into his brain. This version is obviously Middle America's revenge for the beehive hairdo story.

A recent variant tells of a young man who passes out on the floor of a disco. He is found to have put a cucumber in his tight pants to heighten his sex appeal, and it cut off his circulation. Need we discuss the moral here?

There are scores of such stories making the rounds to-day—some long and involved, some quite scary, and most with a buried moral message. Here are a few samples:

A woman fell asleep sunbathing and an ant climbed into her nose and laid eggs in her nasal passages. The eggs hatched, and the itching was so bad that she scratched the flesh off her cheeks.

An older woman had a pet poodle that she was in the habit of drying in a warm oven after she had given him a bath. Someone gave her a microwave oven as a present, and, not realizing how it worked, she tried to dry her poodle in it. You guessed it: she cooked the poor dog to a turn.

Three women from western Pennsylvania made a trip to New York, although they were worried about the crime and violence associated with the city. When they got on the elevator at their hotel, a large black man with a huge dog followed them on. They pressed their backs up against the wall and tried not to act scared, but, when the man said, "Sit" to his dog, they all sat, too. He laughed and introduced himself as Reggie Jackson. After they had recovered themselves, he gave them front-row tickets to a Yankees game. (A reporter asked Jackson about this story, and he said that though he'd heard it hundreds of times, it never really happened. He has never owned a dog in New York.)

A woman left a party alone in her car late at night. As she was driving home, she noticed another car following her. It would pull up close behind her and flash the high beams on and off. She was terrified, as the roads were deserted and she couldn't think how to get help. The car kept following her, sometimes pulling up very close, all the way to her house. As she pulled in her own driveway, she put her hand on the horn. Her husband came running out to see what was the

51

matter just as the driver of the following car rushed up and dragged a man holding a knife out of the back seat of the woman's car. It seems that every time the man in the back seat had raised his knife to stab the woman, the pursuing driver had pulled up close and scared him back down.

Folklorists call this type of extended rumor an "urban legend." The stories are longer than most of the rumors in this book, and they aren't usually attached to a specific product or famous personality, as rumors so often are. But they are related as truth and carried on by word of mouth exactly as the shorter rumors are, and so the distinction becomes somewhat blurry. A good book on urban legends is *The Vanishing Hitchhiker,* by Jan Harold Brunvand.

★ ★ A couple went out on a date last summer to a drive-in movie, and picked up some take-out fried chicken on the way. As they were eating the chicken in the car, the woman said she thought hers tasted funny. The man was too busy eating and watching the movie to bother and told his date the chicken was fine. When they were almost done, she finally turned on the light in the car and found out that she'd been eating a fried rat. She is suing the take-out restaurant for thousands of dollars. (1960s)

Not true. This is another urban legend, easily identified as such by the unchanging form of the story—the woman is always the one who gets the rat, and she always eats most of it in dim light before discovering the problem. In another version she is too busy to cook dinner, and so picks up some take-out chicken, which she and her husband eat at home by candlelight. A moral is often attached to this last version with a "she got what she deserved" ending—implying that women should take the time to cook dinner themselves. It is possible that the legend has its roots in actual cases of fried rats, but it has taken on a story form quite independent of fact.

Another food-contamination story features a woman who thought her soft drink tasted strange. She looked in the bottom of the bottle and discovered a badly decomposed mouse. According to the story, the bottling company has paid her ten thousand dollars to keep the matter quiet. This is a common story, which probably *is* derived from actual cases, though the popular version seems to fixate unfairly on Coca-Cola. There have been lawsuits revolving around parts of mice found in all sorts of soft-drink bottles. Gary Allen Fine, a folklore professor at the University of Minnesota, checked the records of state appellate courts and found forty-five such cases between 1914 and 1976—and these are only the cases that were tried and appealed. There is no way of knowing how many cases have been settled out of court, or have ended after the lower court's ruling. Clearly, people do sometimes find mice in their soft drinks, and they do sometimes win damages in court for their trauma—though rarely as much money as the stories claim.

★ ★ Food inspectors allow up to two rat hairs in each Grade A hot dog.

Not true. Any meat sold for human consumption, including hot dogs, must go through a series of inspections by U.S. Department of Agriculture inspectors—first of the animals before slaughter, then of the dressed meat, and finally of the meat as prepared for packaging. The inspectors' job is to ensure that the meat you buy is free of any contamination or imperfection. However, given the nature of high-speed methods of food processing, the Department of Agriculture concedes that it is not impossible for some contamination, such as a few rodent hairs, to come into contact with the meat. It is up to an individual inspector to spot contamination and to decide at what point the foreign matter renders the meat unacceptable.

The Food and Drug Administration, which oversees the inspection of foods other than meat, offers its inspectors a guide to where the line should be drawn. Every year it prints a table of "food defect action levels" for the many products under its control. Inspectors are instructed to reject any food that might be a hazard to health if consumed and to refer to the tables only if the food seems otherwise satisfactory.

The action level for frozen broccoli, to give an example, is an average of sixty aphids, thrips, and/or mites per hundred grams, or roughly two hundred in a twelve-ounce package. (Remember that aphids, thrips, and mites are very tiny bugs and not at all harmful if eaten.) A thirty-two-ounce can of tomato juice would be considered acceptable if it contained no more than seventeen fruit-fly eggs or one and a half maggots. (Again, keep in mind that a fruit fly is a very small creature.) A one-ounce package of ground paprika is assigned an action level of eighty-two insect fragments or twelve rodent hairs. For a one-ounce tin of curry powder the level is one hundred ten insect fragments or four rodent hairs. Other levels, some of them much lower than these, have been designated for virtually every food grown and processed for human consumption.

The FDA explains the necessity for these action levels very reasonably:

> The action levels are set because it is not now possible, and never has been possible, to grow in open fields, harvest, and process crops that are totally free of natural defects. The alternative to establishing natural defect levels in some foods would be to insist on increased utilization of chemical substances to control insects, rodents, and other natural contaminants. The alternative is not satisfactory because of the very real danger of exposing consumers to potential hazards from residues of these chemicals as opposed to the aesthetically unpleasant, but harmless natural and unavoidable defects.

The FDA emphasizes that the action levels apply only to food that is otherwise healthy and that has been processed under sanitary conditions using good current manufacturing practice. Any number of other factors could lead an inspector to reject a batch of food at well below the set defect level.

★ ★ The breakfast cereal Force contains morphine. (1940s)

Not true. The manufacturer offered cash rewards in an effort to track down the source of this rumor, but the culprit was never apprehended. Had the rumor begun twenty years later, when people were actively searching for drug-laced products, the sale of Force might have been helped by the story—eating cereal for a high would have been easier than smoking banana peels and inhaling aerosol whipped cream! But morphine was definitely not on a mother's list of breakfast foods back in the forties, and the cereal suffered sales setbacks despite vigorous denials from the company.

★ ★ Absinthe is an anti-aphrodisiac, and is responsible for France's population decline. (1908)

Not true. France's population did decline slightly in the decade before World War I, and the drop in the birth rate coincided with a fervent worldwide movement for the prohibition of alcohol. As a popular and very strong drink—68 percent alcohol by volume—absinthe served as the first major target for the temperance crusade in Europe. The rumor fit nicely with the beliefs of the prohibitionists, and it served their cause well, in spite of the fact that it was completely without foundation.

The rumor was so widespread for a time that a legend even grew up about its origin—this story designed to satisfy the pro-absinthe forces. According to the tale, a blackmailer approached Pernod Fils, the major absinthe producer, with a plan to start a rumor attack against the drink. He detailed a list of dangerous qualities that he was prepared to pin on absinthe—qualities sure to scare off Pernod's customers. He also explained that he was prepared to drop his plan without another word if Pernod paid him the price he asked. The distiller refused, and the blackmailer went into action. Soon, tongues all over France were wagging about the frightening effects of absinthe. Pernod, realizing that they should have accepted the blackmailer's offer, tracked him down and offered him even more money to undo his work. He took the money and tried every method of reversing the effects of his smear campaign, but his stories had taken such a firm hold that nothing he did could silence them.

Both stories contributed to the hysteria surrounding the fight over the prohibition of absinthe. At first the debate centered on the drink's high alcohol content and the fact that it was commonly drunk as an aperitif, before meals. Alcohol taken on an empty stomach is absorbed into the bloodstream faster and more completely than a drink taken after or during a meal. But before long, the attack turned to other aspects of the drink, most notably its wormwood content. Of all the flavorings in absinthe—among them anise, peppermint, coriander, hyssop, citron peel, and licorice root—wormwood has the strongest effect on the body. Wormwood oil was prescribed at the time as an anti-spasmodic for epileptics, and large doses were known to have a powerful effect on the nervous system.

Though absinthe contained only a very small amount of wormwood as a flavoring, the anti-absinthe crusaders soon focused their energies on those few drops in each bottle, claiming that the herb made absinthe addictive, and—even worse—that it caused madness. Two cases were cited repeatedly—an absinthe "fiend" who shot and killed a well-known Parisian actor, and an absinthe-maddened laborer who charged around a village just outside Paris one night brandishing a knife until a child stunned him with a rock thrown at his forehead. The *London Times*'s Paris correspondent called absinthe "a poison more powerful in murderous impulse than any other. . . . It insinuates itself . . . and acts directly upon the nervous system."

Absinthe was outlawed in Switzerland and Belgium in 1908, and, with the excess supply of the liquor that then flooded France from those countries, came the full fury of the anti-absinthe campaign. It turned out to be a protracted battle. Absinthe made up 30 percent of the liquor consumed in France in those years, and people accustomed to the drink were not willing to give it up easily. During the early days of World War I, a rumor circulated in the United States to the effect that French officers filled their soldiers with absinthe to give them courage in battle. This could not have been further from the truth. Military leaders early in the war became disgusted at the drunken state in which some of their new recruits arrived and pushed for a nationwide ban on absinthe to insure a better quality of soldiery. It was largely through this military pressure that absinthe was finally outlawed in 1915.

The curious will be glad to hear that absinthe hasn't completely disappeared. Today Pernod Fils makes much the same drink, minus the wormwood, and sells it under the name Pernod.

★ ★ You can get high from smoking dried banana peels. (1967)

Not true. Smoking banana peels—"mellow yellow" to insiders—may make you cough, and, if you cough enough, you may start to feel a little dizzy, but the fact is that if you slipped on one you'd probably go higher. At best, smoking banana peels is an inexpensive and unilluminating diversion. We have never run across anyone who tried it more than once.

Drug-related rumors were rampant in the sixties. They told of common household products and groceries that could be turned into drugs and of secret drug messages in popular songs. Peter, Paul, and Mary's "Puff the Magic Dragon" was rumored to be a marijuana ballad, and Donovan's "Mellow Yellow" was said to be the official theme song for banana smokers. The speculation about the meaning behind such songs was heightened by the obscure lyrics of some songs that actually were about drugs—songs like the Beatles' "Lucy in the Sky with Diamonds," the Jefferson Airplane's "White Rabbit," and the Byrds' "Eight Miles High."

Most of the household-hint-type drug rumors told of everyday foods and products that took on unusual properties when smoked—items like turnip greens, catnip, and cigarettes soaked in cough syrup. The worm at the bottom of a tequila bottle was said to give mild hallucinations when eaten. (Tequila is not bottled with a worm, though a similar drink, mescal, is. Both liquors are made from the leaves of maguey plants, not from the mescal cactus, the source of the hallucinogen mescaline.)

Some of the drug rumors of the sixties turn out to have a basis in pharmacology. We never thought much of the claim that nutmeg can be eaten for a high, but it appears to be the truth. Taken in large doses it can produce a 24-hour reaction that includes nausea, dehydration, hallucinations, and after-effects characterized by pains throughout the body. The spice was taken in such large quantities mainly by people who had no other drugs available to them. Morning glory seeds also have hallucinogenic properties, and researchers have found the causative chemical to be very similar in structure to LSD. Spanish explorers recorded that Aztec priests swallowed the seeds in order to receive visions from their gods. Harvard students revived the practice in 1963 when they discovered that pulverized seeds stirred into a milkshake produced tasty and colorful results. The seeds of the Aztecs are now known to gardeners as the varieties Heavenly Blue and Pearly Gates.

Though those two stories turn out to have a basis in fact, we need hardly emphasize that most of these cheap-drug rumors are pure myth, and some may be dangerous. A harmless one for the truly desperate maintains that drinking the cigarette ashes at the bottom of a can of beer will produce a high. At least one of the beer-drinking rumors of the sixties has survived to make the rounds among today's teenagers—that you will get drunk faster if you drink beer through a straw. It's not true, but it apparently sounds plausible enough to have become a permanent part of drinking lore.

Rock musicians frequently did indulge in drugs and alcohol, either to prime themselves for performances or to maintain an image of decadence. Alice Cooper, for instance, used to drink a case of beer a day, and the cost of beer for his band ran to thousands of dollars in 1974. But rumors went beyond the actual exploits and told of the rock stars' reputed secret habits. One that intrigued us was that Jimi

Hendrix put tabs of LSD under his bandana before a concert, and as he worked up a sweat during the performance, the drug slowly percolated through his skin. On a healthy note, we also heard that Janis Joplin prepared for her concerts by eating a dozen lemons—hence her contorted face and raspy voice.

★ ★ Green M & Ms make you horny. (1970s)

Not true. Or maybe true if you are *highly* suggestible. The Mars Company of Hacketstown, New Jersey, makers of plain M & Ms since 1941 and peanut M & Ms since 1954, vigorously denies that green M & Ms have any libido-heightening properties. Mars has no idea how this rumor got started, and neither do we. But we have seen people wearing tee shirts that say "Green M & Ms Make You Horny," and the company, which takes the rumor with good humor, must frequently deny requests to make custom packages of green-only M & Ms.

A mutation of this rumor has it that red M & Ms disappeared from the market because they were such a potent aphrodisiac that employees pocketed them before they made it off the production line. This isn't true either. Red M & Ms vanished—along with bright pink hot dogs and certain lipstick colors—in 1976 when the Food and Drug Administration cracked down on the use of Red Dye #2. The loss of red M & Ms saddened many candy lovers, and in 1983 the most disconsolate among them banded together to advocate their return.

A 1984 package of plain M & Ms contains 40% brown, 20% yellow, 20% orange, 10% tan, and 10% green candies, and a package of peanut M & Ms contains equal proportions of brown, yellow, green, and orange candies—color balances that the Mars company has arrived at after extensive research into consumer preferences.

★ ★ Girls can avoid pregnancy by jumping up and down after sex.

Not true. Rumors designed to make children and adolescents feel uncomfortable about their bodies are a genre unto themselves. The litany of horrors seems endless: girls shouldn't wear patent leather shoes because they reflect what's under their skirts; they shouldn't wear white dresses because they remind boys of bed sheets; if they wear short skirts, they risk contracting polio. You shouldn't wear rubber boots indoors because your feet will shrink; if you bite your fingernails a hand will grow in your stomach; if you swallow a watermelon seed a watermelon will grow in your stomach; if you masturbate, you'll go blind or crazy or both; if you have sex, your pimples will go away; sex *causes* pimples; if you squeeze pimples in certain strategic places on your face your brain can become infected (we saw a slide show about this in health class); you can get pregnant from swimming pools, and from semen *on your stomach*; you won't get pregnant if you have sex standing up; and you won't get pregnant the first time you have sex.

All these horror stories are hogwash, but they and others like them torment every generation. Is it any wonder that so many adults need to consult psychiatrists?

★ ★ If you find a Tootsie Roll Pop candy wrapper with a picture of a little Indian warrior aiming his bow and arrow at a star, the company will send you a free bag of the candies. (Since 1936)

Not true. This rumor has attached itself to Tootsie Roll Pops for decades—since the candies were first introduced in 1936. It's a nice idea, but unfortunately that's about all it is. The company has never exchanged candy for the Indian wrappers—if it did, it would quickly find itself giving away more candy than it sold. Our own statistical analysis revealed that close to half of all Toot-

sie Roll Pop wrappers show the little Indian. (No need to pity us our work—the candies are every bit as tasty and chewy as we remembered them.)

Tootsie Roll Industries doesn't enjoy the unpleasant chore of disappointing its young customers with bad news, so in response to inquiries it sends out an intriguing letter, stamped "Secret," with an even stranger explanation of the Indian wrapper. This official version tells how—long, long ago—a great Indian chief named Shooting Star showed a struggling candy-maker how to put a delicious chewy center in his lollipops. The chief occasionally comes back to see that the suckers are still being made according to formula, and the Indian on the wrapper is a sign that he personally checked that candy.

We have to hand it to Tootsie Roll for creatively fighting fire with fire. If the company can get away with sending a wild legend to children who are hoping for free candy, more power to it. Maybe children accept the Chief Shooting Star legend as truth and give up their expectation of a handout without a fuss, but we, for two, were left less than satisfied.

Free candy stories seem to be the childhood parallel to the car-for-a-penny rumors of later life. Another wishful tale holds that a certain brand of candy bar sometimes comes with a number printed on the wrapper, and that the company will trade one of these wrappers for a whole carton of candy. This one has come and gone for generations, fixing on different candy bars as it evolves. Some of the bars always bear a number on their wrapper. Some never do. But the story was a myth from its conception. At best it serves as rumor training for the young, teaching them that they shouldn't believe everything they hear.

★ ★ Appetite suppressant candies contain worm eggs, which hatch in the stomach and eat the food there, thus causing weight loss. (1960s)

Not true. The active ingredient in most appetite-supressant candies is benzocaine, a local anesthetic that numbs the stomach and quells hunger pangs. One candy is supposed to be taken a short time before each meal, in order to make not eating a little less painful.

★ ★ Coca-Cola is made with cocaine. (1930s)

Not true. This little tidbit is a key element in the mythology surrounding the world's most popular and mysterious soft drink. It *is* true that the earliest version of the drink, the Coca-Cola sold at soda fountains in the 1880s and '90s, did contain a weak dose of the drug. The Coca-Cola Company is today understandably sensitive about that early formula. Their official line: "If Coca-Cola ever contained cocaine, and we do not acknowledge that it did, it was only in trace amounts." In fact, the early drink was advertised as an "exhilarating" mixture of the kola nut—a plant rich in caffeine—and the coca leaf—the natural source of cocaine. Beverages made from the coca leaf were popular at the time, and Coca-Cola, as the best tasting of the drinks available, was soon in great demand. But by 1905, in response to mounting public sentiment against the use of addictive drugs in patent medicines, the company changed the formula of the drink, and has since used only decocainized coca leaves in the beverage as a flavoring agent.

Yet the memory of the drink of the 1890s has lingered on, especially in the South, where for many years Coca-Cola was nicknamed "dope"—also the slang term for cocaine. Jean Stafford, in a wonderful reminiscence about Coca-Cola published in *Esquire* magazine in 1975, tells how her mother warned her away from the drink and cautioned her *never* to accept a glass from a stange man—an aspirin dropped in a glass of Coke was rumored to be a sure-fire knockout formula. (This combination was still believed potent in the 1960s, when it was said that Coke and aspirin would make you high.) So magical was the drink considered, that college students relied on it for just the opposite effect—mixed with ammonia it was taken as an "upper" during final exams. It was even thought by some to be an effective contraceptive when used as a douche. All these beliefs, of course, are false. Coca-Cola's chief active ingredients are carbonated water, sugar, caffeine, caramel, and phosphoric acid.

The Coca-Cola Company may have indirectly fueled rumors by cloaking the drink's formula in secrecy. Since the first bottle of Coke was made in 1885, only a handful of key personnel have known the full recipe. Even today the mysterious syrup that flavors Coca-Cola around the world is prepared in Atlanta, Georgia, by trusted employees, each of whom knows only part of the recipe.

We have heard that a southern tradition of cooking has grown up around Coca-Cola—that hams are basted in the drink, and that it is the main ingredient in a particular molded salad. But, as we have never met anyone who has made or even tasted one of these delicacies, we must assume these are more wild rumors.

★ ★ Dr. Pepper is made with prune juice.

Not true. According to a company spokesperson, "Dr. Pepper does not, nor has it ever contained prune juice or any prune flavorings." This rumor has been around for generations, and the company gently refutes it in a brochure it sends to curious consumers. The text contains this statement: "There are 23 flavors and other ingredients (none of which are prunes) that produce the inimitable taste of Dr. Pepper." The company doesn't know exactly why or when the prune-juice rumor surfaced, but the story could have been inspired by Dr. Pepper's vaguely "fruity" taste and is just the sort of message that certain children like to repeat in order to alarm other children.

Like the Coca-Cola Company, the Dr. Pepper Company may have inadvertently helped to sustain this rumor by surrounding its formula with mystery. The Dr. Pepper recipe is divided into two parts, each of which is locked up in a different Dallas bank so that no single person can ever be in possession of the whole formula.

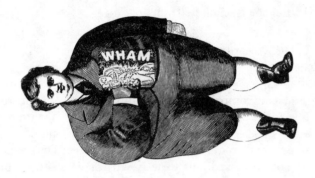

★ ★ Pop Rocks and Coca-Cola are a lethal combination. Their most famous victim was Mikey, the little brother on the Life cereal commercials. (1978)

Not true. This is an example of a childhood-bravery rumor—in this case spread by children to make themselves feel courageous when they eat Pop Rocks. General Foods hired a public relations agency to help stamp out the story and its simpler and more damaging version: that Pop Rocks alone will make your stomach explode.

The stories are of course completely untrue. Pop Rocks is a harmless and amusing candy that fizzles mildly when wet. And Mikey is still very much alive. He may be a perpetual three-year-old in the Life commercial, but in real life he will be sixteen this year. His real name is John Gilchrist, and he has done some acting since the Life ad, but is now concentrating on getting through high school. (Incidentally, we discovered that the two older brothers in the television ad are John's real brothers, Tommy and Michael.)

The child-as-victim story can attack and cripple with equal ease a promising new product or a time-tested favorite—the kind of product a company relies on as the backbone of its economic health. In 1977, Life Savers found itself battling a strange but cruelly damaging rumor—that a chewing gum the company had introduced with great success was made with spider eggs. As this falsehood spread—and it traveled with alarming speed—it picked up the added assertion that the gum caused cancer. The gum was an important new product for Life Savers—it had been promoted at some expense and had found itself a very successful niche in the bubble-gum market—so the company did what any of us might do in a similar situation. It went on the attack. Full-page advertisements appeared in newspapers across the country with the headline "Somebody is telling your kids very bad lies about a very good gum." (That somebody was, of course, the kids themselves.) According to the *Wall Street Journal,* the company spent between $50,000 and $100,000 fighting the rumors.

The stories eventually died down, though we will never know if their demise was the result of Life Savers' efforts. Rumors seem to have a natural life span, and the policy most experts recommend in fighting them involves silence, patience, and truthful answers to any inquiries.

★ ★ McDonald's hamburgers contain spider eggs. (1978)

Not true. Does something sound familiar here? This is an example of a rumor that jumped its track—from bubble gum to hamburgers. Where did people think all those spider eggs came from, anyway? Spider farms? (An unrelated rumor from the twenties accused the more exclusive wine stores of employing spiders to make their bottles appear old and cobwebbed.)

McDonald's had come under fire in 1977 with a groundless rumor that it was funding a Satanic cult, and executives were just feeling safe again with that story under control, when a whole new batch of trouble started—this time about the unwholesome substances in the hamburgers. The rumors claimed that in order to boost their burgers' protein content, McDonald's was mixing spider eggs, worms, or kangaroo meat with the beef—earthworms was the additive most often cited. All of the stories, of course, are untrue. The company thinks the story started in Chattanooga, Tennessee, but they have no idea how or why. For a time their advertisements stressed that all their hamburgers were made with 100 percent pure beef. Before fading away, the rumor attached itself to several of the other hamburger chains as well.

If you have heard that McDonald's milkshakes are made with seaweed, you heard the truth. The shakes contain carrageenan, made from the seaweed carrageen, used in many foods as a thickening agent and of particular importance to the milkshake formula, because it controls the growth of ice crystals and keeps the shake liquid. You will also find carrageenan on the list of ingredients in most ice creams.

If you heard and believed that Dairy Queen ice cream is made from lignite, or drilling mud, there's probably nothing we can do to help you. This, of course, is a joke rumor, told more as jest than as fact. It was never believable enough to travel far.

★ ★ As a child, Humphrey Bogart was the model for the Gerber baby. (1940s)

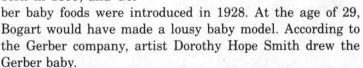

Not true. This rumor arose because Bogart's mother was a commercial illustrator, who *may* have done some illustrating for baby products. Bogart was born in 1899, and Gerber baby foods were introduced in 1928. At the age of 29, Bogart would have made a lousy baby model. According to the Gerber company, artist Dorothy Hope Smith drew the Gerber baby.

This rumor lives on as an item of movie lore in spite of its proven falsity. We last saw it printed in a personality fact column in the *Boston Globe* in the fall of 1982.

★ ★ Rock Hudson and Jim Nabors were secretly married. (1960s)

Not true. This rumor was started by a group of Malibu pranksters, who sent out fake wedding invitations as a joke. The story has since spread as a full-fledged and enduring rumor, though it is entirely false. Neither of the stars is particularly fond of the rumor. Hudson could not even manage a smile over a recent *Harvard Lampoon* parody announcing the pair's divorce. When asked by a *People Magazine* reporter about the joke he gave only an icy "no comment."

The Hollywood rumor mill has made a lot of scandalous accusations that, though almost always untrue, have managed to smudge the good names of many actors and actresses. Other falsely paired couples over the years have included Cary Grant and Randolph Scott (they shared a beach house in the thirties), and Lana Turner and Ava Gardner. All these scandalous alleged couplings have been publicized by fan magazines that pay handsomely for titillating gossip without bothering to check its accuracy.

★ ★ Sonny and Cher are both women. (1969)

Not true. In a 1975 *Playboy* interview, Cher rated this the most outrageous story she ever heard about herself and said that she and Sonny had "a really good laugh" over it. The bellbottomed couple were also rumored to be brother and sister. They are not.

★ ★ Michael Jackson sang the high notes for Diana Ross on several of her recordings. (1982)

Not true. Michael Jackson has found himself the object of a barrage of outrageous rumors in the last couple of years, probably for the simple reason that his songs have hit the top of the music charts and brought him wide public exposure. He is also wrongly rumored to be the illegitimate son of Diana Ross (you can tell by the facial structure, say the whisperers) and, wilder yet, to be Donna Summer in drag. Donna Summer is herself falsely rumored to be a transsexual, originally named Donald, who had a sex-change operation in Germany several years ago. Now, let's see . . . that would make Michael Jackson a previously male female impersonating a male. Or something like that. All these stories are untrue.

★ ★ Robert Young went blind after he finished playing Marcus Welby on the television series. You can tell because in the Sanka commercials he always has his hand on someone. (1982)

Not true. This one rates several stars for sheer silliness. It also richly demonstrates the power that a mere suggestion of evidence—"because in the Sanka commercials he always has his hand on someone"—adds to a rumor. The untrue rumor that Mae West had a wooden leg was usually bolstered in the same way ("You can tell because she always wears long dresses"), as was the untrue joke-rumor that Walter Cronkite has no legs ("You can tell because CBS never shows him standing up.")

★ ★ Jerry Mathers, who played Beaver on the television series "Leave It To Beaver," died in action in Vietnam. (1968)

Not true. This is a classic sixties rumor—it summed up so precisely what had happened to the country in that decade, or so we thought. Beaver was the all-American kid from the all-American suburban home, the kid we'd all admired on television—and he'd grown up like everybody else and gotten himself shot in Vietnam. It was just too much. It somehow proved that clean-cut all-American living didn't get you very far.

But Jerry Mathers didn't die in Vietnam. He never even *went* to Vietnam. He's still alive and well and acting in southern California. In fact he, with most of the rest of the original cast, acted in a 1983 CBS movie sequel to "Leave It To Beaver"—with Beaver now a thirty-four-year-old divorced father who comes home with his two sons to sort out his life.

When asked about the rumor, Mathers likes to recite Mark Twain's famous line: "The reports of my death are greatly exaggerated." Both AP and UPI carried the story of his death in 1968, and when they discovered the mistake, each wire service blamed the other. After that, the story was carried on by word of mouth.

Beaver's death was not the only rumor to come out of "Leave It To Beaver." We also heard in 1972 that rock star Alice Cooper had, as a youth, played Wally's friend Eddie Haskell on the show. Cooper himself started this one—it was just one of the many stories he told to keep his fans guessing about his true identity. He made the claim for a while at his news conferences, then grew tired of the idea and announced that he was actually the illegitimate son of baseball player Jimmy Piersall. He has since suggested that he and Liza Minnelli are the same person.

"Leave It To Beaver" grown up: From left to right: Ken Osmond (who played Eddie Haskell), Tony Dow (Wally), Barbara Billingsley (June), and Jerry Mathers (Beaver).

Just as we thought we'd straightened out the Beaver stories, we heard in 1973 that Ken Osmond, the actor who really *did* play Eddie Haskell on the show, had gone on to become a star of pornographic movies. Give us a break! Osmond works today as a Los Angeles police officer. The source of the rumor seems to have been an eight-millimeter porno film starring John Holmes—"Long John" to his fans. The film was released with the announcement that Holmes had once played "little Eddie Haskell" on "Leave It To Beaver." We can only think that whoever wrote that copy must have been desperate for something nice to say about Holmes, because the statement came right out of the blue sky. Holmes never even had a bit part on "Leave It To Beaver," and he was *not* invited to play in the 1983 movie sequel.

Lest you think that all of the rumors about "Leave It To Beaver" were bad, we also heard that Lumpy Rutherford, the loser kid from down the block, grew up to marry Raquel Welch. We're sorry to report that this is just another Beaver myth. The same story is sometimes told about Wally.

One last Beaver tale maintained that after the final episode of the series was filmed, June (Barbara Billingsley) had to have her pearls surgically removed.

★ ★ The Ivory Snow mother, pictured on the detergent box holding a baby, has gone on to become a star of pornographic movies. (1970s)

True. Marilyn Chambers, whose picture graced the Ivory Snow box in the early seventies, went on to become the star of *Behind the Green Door* and several other not-so-pure movies. When her first film came out, Chambers told the press that her new fame ought to "sell a lot more soap." The detergent box with her likeness is now a sought-after collectible.

★ ★ Maynard G. Krebbs died when a radio fell in his bathtub. (1963)

Not true. Bob Denver, who played the character of Maynard G. Krebbs on the television series "The Many Loves of Dobie Gillis," is still alive. The rumor started after the show went off the air and ended suddenly when Denver showed up in 1964 on "Gilligan's Island." Many people who believed the story still remember it with a strange fondness.

The "Dobie Gillis" show was a classic of late-fifties television, and it had a devoted following. Maynard G. Krebbs (the "G.", he once confided, stood for William) was an appealing beatnik with a pathological aversion to work. He served as foil and "good buddy" to the driven Dobie (played

77

by Dwayne Hickman). Other regulars on the series included Tuesday Weld (as Thalia Menninger) and Warren Beatty (as Milton Armitage).

★ ★ Fidel Castro worked as an extra in Hollywood during the early forties, and can be seen in several Xavier Cugat movies— including *Two Girls and a Sailor* and *Holiday in Mexico*.

Not true. Fidel Castro first travelled to the United States in 1948, when he and his wife spent their honeymoon in Miami. During the years that he is supposed to have worked on the Cugat musicals he was in fact enrolled as a student in Havana— from 1942 to 1945 at the Jesuit College of Belen, and from then until 1950 as a law student at the University of Havana. While few details are known about Castro's life as a student, it is certain that he spent no time in Hollywood. As for the possibility that he did some acting in his spare time in Havana, we do have one clue. When he graduated from the College of Belen, his teachers added his name to the school's honor roll with an intriguing note: "He has good qualities, and is something of an actor."

The story of Castro's Hollywood days probably grew out of bandleader Xavier Cugat's cryptic recollection of a dancer he once hired. Cugat began to serenade Los Angeles audiences with his Latin rhythms in 1929, as the leader of a band called the Gigolos. He soon found that Californians needed encouragement before they would attempt such unfamiliar dances as the rumba or the samba. So Cugat hired dancers to get them started, and with uncanny foresight he picked a group who would later go on to fame and fortune—among them Rita Hayworth, Ramon Ramos, and Eddie LeBaron. In a 1943 interview for *Colliers* magazine, Cugat mentioned another of his early dancers whose name he thought it best to leave unsaid, "since he is at the moment a South American general." This passing remark, made while Fidel Castro was still a young student in Havana, may well be the origin of the rumor that was to surface years later. Cugat makes no further reference to the dancer-general in his 1948 autobiography, *Rumba Is My Life*, but he does discuss his acquaintance in the early thirties with a man who was to become a powerful figure in Cuba—General Benitez, later a key supporter of General Fulgencio Batista, the dictator Castro overthrew in 1959. Could General Benitez have been the mysterious rumba dancer, we wonder? The true source of the Castro-in-Hollywood stories? We will probably never know for sure.

Another often-told story about Castro very nearly puts him in training camp for the New York Yankees. According to this rumor, Castro was scouted as a possible pitcher by several major league baseball teams while he was a college player in Havana. If we believe this one, we give our American baseball teams the power to change the course of history. (If only they'd made an offer!) The Yankees' scouting department doesn't have any record of looking Fidel over, but the scouts admit they might have watched him without knowing who he was. Many teams were actively scouting in Cuba during the forties, and if Castro so much as pitched a game he might have been noticed by one of them. Castro was an athletic student—he distinguished himself in basketball, swimming, and track—but unfortunately we can't say for certain that he has ever played baseball.

★ ★ "Mama" Cass Elliot of the Mamas and the Papas singing group choked to death on a ham sandwich. (1974)

Not true. But she did die in 1974, and you aren't completely flaky if you remember reading this in the news. The *New York Times,* in its first report of her death, wrote: "Her physician says she probably choked on a sandwich." *Rolling Stone* printed much the same story. Not until a week later did the official coroner's report deny the ham-sandwich theory and conclude that Elliot had died of a heart attack brought on by obesity. She weighed about 220 pounds, roughly twice the healthy weight for a woman of her height. There was also a ridiculous rumor that at the time of her death she was pregnant by John Lennon. The coroner's report never mentioned anything about *that*.

Incidentally, the average size piece of meat responsible for choking deaths is about the size of a cigarette package.

★ ★ Catherine the Great of Russia had an immense sexual appetite which led to her death when a horse was lowered on her too suddenly.

Not true. The Empress suffered an attack of apoplexy at the age of sixty-seven, while sitting on her commode, and died in her bed two days later.

Catherine reached the throne in 1762 by overthrowing her husband, Peter III, who died in prison not long after. With no husband to restrain her, the Empress amused herself with a steady stream of lovers during her thirty-four year reign, mostly handsome young army officers. French historians, writing with a clear anti-Russian bias, later built these affairs into a legend of debauchery that has attached itself firmly to Catherine's memory. From the French writers came the story that her lovers were all examined by a palace doctor

81

before being admitted to her bed, so great was her fear of venereal disease. Also French, and unconfirmed by any first-hand Russian sources, is the myth that the Empress employed a trusted aide to test and approve her choices. Two women of Catherine's court, Countess Bruce and Madame Protasova, have been unfairly labeled *les eprouveuses*—the testers.

While Catherine's sexual appetite was admittedly large, it did not require staff assistance, and it did *not* run to horses. An item of rumor lore often told to back up the legend of her death is equally false: that in the depths of the Kremlin Armory in Moscow sit the horseshoes worn by Catherine's favorite steed. According to the tale, they are made of pure silver, forged in the shape of hearts.

★ ★ Paul McCartney is dead. (1969)

Not true. This rumor spread like wildfire among Beatles fans in October and November 1969, shortly after the release of the Album "Abbey Road." The story seems to have started in the Midwest. The first printed account in the Illinois University newspaper, the *Northern Star* on September 23, cryptically cites its source as "a midwestern university" where "there has been much conjecturing on the present state of Beatle Paul McCartney." Those conjectures were quickly picked up and expanded upon in other student papers and on the radio waves of rock-and-roll stations. The full story was that McCartney had died in November 1966 in a car accident outside London and that a double had secretly taken his place. Believers in the rumor had a barrage of evidence to back them up, from the fact of Paul's absence from the public eye—the Beatles had not been on a concert tour since 1966, and at Bob Dylan's huge Isle of Wight concert in August 1969 the other three Beatles had appeared without Paul—to an encyclopedia of minute suggestions in the Beatles' music and album designs. It seemed the group had left a trail of clues for their fans to find. Included here are some of the more popular ones:

• When the song "Revolution Number 9," from the "White Album," is played backwards, the words "turn me on, dead man" and "cherish the dead" can be heard, along with the sound of a violent car crash.

• John's voice can be heard to say, "I buried Paul" at the end of the song "Strawberry Fields Forever" on the "Magical Mystery Tour" album. His voice can be made clearer by speeding up the turntable to forty-five rpms.

• On the cover of their "Sergeant Pepper" album, a grave is shown, on which a patch of yellow flowers is arranged in the shape of a left-handed guitar—Paul was the only left-handed

The floral guitar on the grave

member of the group—or possibly the letter "P." On the inside cover Paul wears a black armpatch with the letters "OPD," said to stand for "Officially Pronounced Dead," and a medal on his chest commemorating his death. On the back cover of the album all the Beatles except Paul are facing forward, while Paul has his back turned. An even closer inspection of the photograph—which has been overprinted with the lyrics to the songs on the album—reveals George subtly pointing to the phrase "Wednesday morning at five o'clock," reputedly the time and day of Paul's fatal accident.

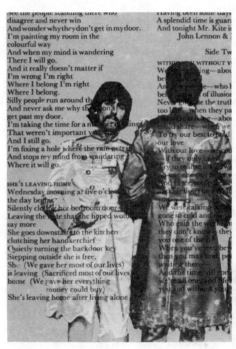

Paul's back and George's pointing finger

The armpatch

The medal

• On the "Abbey Road" album cover the four Beatles are shown in symbolic funeral dress. John, dressed in white, is the minister; Ringo, in black, is the undertaker; George, in work clothes, is the gravedigger; and Paul, barefoot in a suit, is clearly the corpse. Great significance was also read into the fact that McCartney is walking out of step with the others; that he holds a cigarette in his right hand, though he was known to be left-handed; and that the license plate on the Volkswagen behind them reads "28 IF"—twenty-eight being the age Paul would have been in 1969 *if* he had survived the car crash.

The "Abbey Road" album cover.

• In a photograph inside the "Magical Mystery Tour" album cover Paul is wearing a black carnation, while the others wear red flowers, and in another photograph a hand can be

The hands over Paul's head:

On "Magical Mystery Tour"   On "Sergeant Pepper"

seen over his head—an ancient sign of death. Also deemed important was the fact that of the four animals shown on the front cover only the walrus is black. This, combined with other clues—such as the line in the song "Glass Onion," where John sings "Here's another clue for all: the walrus is Paul," and Paul's song "I Am the Walrus"—seemed again to show that Paul was dead. Some claimed that the walrus was a death symbol to the Vikings.

• On a more optimistic note, many believed that a telephone number was hidden on the cover of the "Magical Mystery Tour" album, visible only in a mirror. Rumor had it that if this number was dialed in London at exactly five o'clock on a Wednesday morning, and the caller told enough of the secret to whoever answered, he would be invited to a magical Beatle island in the Mediterranean.

The clues went on and on, and, while searchers were excitedly uncovering more of them, the rumor raged. But, when the number of plausible new discoveries began to dwindle, the story began to lose its luster. The believers and clue finders, who at first had seemed to be so tuned in to the true Beatles, began to sound downright tiresome as they repeated the same ideas over and over again. And, after all, Paul was still around. At least he said he was. In his first comment on the rumor to the press he announced, "I'm alive and well. But if I were dead I would be the last to know." As the rumor persisted he gradually lost his humorous outlook. When a *Life* correspondent sought him out in early November, she got a more somber reaction:

It is all bloody stupid. I picked up that O.P.D. badge in Canada. It was a police badge. Perhaps it means Ontario Police Department or something. I was wearing a black flower because they ran out of red ones. It is John, not me, dressed in black on the cover and inside of "Magical Mystery Tour." On "Abbey Road" we were wearing our ordinary clothes. I was walking barefoot because it was a hot day. The Volkswagen just happened to be parked there. Perhaps the rumor started because I haven't been much in the press lately. . . . . Can you spread it around that I am just an ordinary person and want to live in peace?

The one tangible outcome of all the mysterious speculation was that sales of Beatles records soared, and people clamored to hear their songs on the radio. It was even suggested by some that just maybe the Beatles themselves had . . .

No, we won't even discuss it.

★ ★ Rock star Grace Slick put LSD in the water at Tricia Nixon's wedding. (1971)

Not true. Grace Slick almost got into the White House in April 1970 as an unwelcome guest at a tea party given by Tricia for former Finch College students—Slick had attended the school for a short time—but she made the mistake of bringing as her escort the infamous Abbie Hoffman. The pair never even got near an outside spigot, as guards stopped them at the gate. Slick was not invited to Tricia's 1971 wedding.

★ ★ Richard Nixon gave Gerald Ford the presidency in exchange for the pardon. (1974)

Possibly true. Ford's pardon of Nixon came just a month after Nixon resigned from office in August 1974 in the face of a widening investigation of his role in the Watergate break-in and cover-up. We know that Nixon considered several options before making his decision to resign. If he stayed in office, he faced an impeachment vote in Congress, which, if he lost, would mean the forfeit of the pension and benefits otherwise due him as a former president. If he resigned, he faced criminal charges, which, as he recalled in his 1978 memoir, would have "cost millions of dollars and [taken] years to fight in the courts." To lessen the danger of those lawsuits, he and his aides thought seriously about the granting of a presidential pardon.

By the end of July 1974, with impeachment proceedings already looming in the House of Representatives, Nixon asked Alexander Haig, White House chief of staff, to meet with Vice President Ford and warn him to be prepared to take over the presidency within the next several days. Haig and Ford met on August 1, and, according to Ford's later testimony before a House judiciary subcommittee, they did discuss the possibility of a pardon. Haig outlined the options that Nixon was then considering—including the granting of pardons to all the Watergate conspirators and himself before the resignation, as opposed to the more tactful granting of a pardon by his successor after the resignation. Ford testified that "General Haig wanted my views on the various courses of action, as well as my attitude on the options of resignation." While it appears slightly unseemly for Ford to have discussed a pardon at all with Nixon's chief of staff just days before the resignation, Ford has repeatedly denied that the two men struck a deal at the meeting. He says that at the end of their discussion he asked for time to think.

Ford spoke with Haig again late on the night of August 1 in a telephone call about which recollections vary. Ford's chief of staff, Robert T. Hartmann, wrote in his memoirs that Ford discussed the call with him the next day in a meeting at which two other aides, John O. Marsh, Jr., and Bryce Harlow, were present. According to Hartmann, Ford told the men that he had telephoned Haig at 1:30 A.M. to tell him that Nixon should go ahead with whatever he decided to do. According to Ford himself, it was Haig who made the call, and it was only to report that Nixon was still deliberating whether or not to resign.

If any deal was made, it was struck quietly among Ford, Haig, and Nixon. Unless one of them decides to change his public recollection of the discussions held during that summer of transition, history will record the pardon as an act of beneficence by Gerald Ford.

★ ★ Johnny Carson gave out a credit-card number on the "Tonight" show that anyone could use to make free long-distance calls. (1970s)

Not true. The staff of the "Tonight" show is baffled by this rumor, which surfaces periodically and results in streams of phone calls to the show from people who want to know what the number is or say that they have tried the number and that it doesn't work. No one at NBC knows what prompted the story, but it comes in three versions: that Johnny Carson gave out the number because he was mad at the telephone company; that Burt Reynolds gave out the number because he was mad at the telephone company; or that it flashed across the screen during the show.

Another "Tonight"-related rumor popular in the seventies had it that Johnny Carson started the great toilet-paper crisis of 1974 by making a joke during his monologue about an impending toilet-paper shortage. The real story behind that short-lived but hysteria-inducing "shortage" is that in November 1973 a congressman from Wisconsin, responding to complaints from his constituents about a shortage of pulp paper in the state, issued a news release that began: "The

Government Printing Office is facing a serious shortage of paper." Then the congressman discovered that the federal government had fallen behind schedule in obtaining bids to provide bureaucratic bathrooms with their regular supply of toilet paper, and he issued another release that began: "The United States may face a serious shortage of toilet paper within a few months . . . . I hope we don't have to ration toilet tissue . . . ." The press leapt on the story, and, in the ensuing flurry, the qualifying words like "may" and "I hope" got lost. On December 19, Johnny Carson cracked a joke about the alleged "shortage" in his monologue, and the next day viewers, and friends of viewers, and friends of friends of viewers stormed the grocery stores in a frenzied attempt to hoard what toilet paper was available. It didn't help that store managers, appalled at the sight of customers stripping the shelves, posted signs that said "limit two per customer." Later in the week an incredulous Johnny Carson paused for a moment on the show to apologize for his unwitting part in the rumor: "I don't want to be remembered as the man who created a false toilet paper scare," he said. "I just picked up the item from the paper and enlarged it somewhat and made some jokes as to what they could do about it. There's no shortage."

The staff at the "Tonight" show is mystified by another strange tale about the show. According to the story, Johnny had as his guest one night the wife of a famous golfer. During their interview he asked her what little superstitious things she did before a tournament to give her husband good luck. She answered, "I kiss his balls." Supposedly Carson came back with, "That must make his putter stand up." The woman walked off the show in anger. It's a good story, but it never happened.

We'll leave you with one bit of trivia about the "Tonight" show that really is true. Popular singer Paul Anka did compose the show's theme song, "Here's Johnny," and he receives regular royalties from its performance.

★ ★ A children's-television-show host was taken off the air after he said, "That ought to shut the little bastards up!" on live television during what he thought was a commercial break. (1960s)

Not true. The statement was attributed, in different versions of the tale, to virtually every local children's-show host around the country. Despite a complete lack of supporting evidence—no one telling the story had ever seen the episode themselves—the myth was widely believed. Many who heard it as children still consider the story a fact.

This is one example of a genre of rumor told about television personalities who supposedly lost their jobs for making scandalous remarks on the air. Groucho Marx's interview-game show, "You Bet Your Life," was rumored to have been canceled over a lewd joke. According to the legend, Groucho had as a guest a man with twelve children. Groucho asked about the children and suggested that the man must really love his wife. His guest, of course, admitted that yes, he did love his wife very much, to which Groucho allegedly replied, "Well, I love my cigar too, but I take it out once in a while."

According to the story, network executives and censors hit the ceiling, and Groucho was yanked off the air. The truth is much less dramatic. Groucho never made the remark; NBC dropped the show in 1961 because of lackluster ratings.

Such stories are no doubt inspired by the surprising things that sometimes *were* said on television, especially in the days of live broadcasting. Groucho Marx was in fact notorious for his double-edge witticisms. In one interview that really was aired, Groucho asked a father of triplets what he did for a living. The man answered that he worked for the California Power Company, to which Groucho quipped, "My boy, you don't work for the California Power Company. You *are* the California Power Company."

Many statements and jokes made on other game shows had double meanings, whether intended or not. When Sal Mineo appeared as the mystery guest on "What's My Line?", the panel had some trouble guessing his identity. They did figure out that he was an actor and Dorothy Kilgallen tried to narrow it down further by asking, "Are you the kind of leading man who gets the leading lady in the end?" When another panelist burst out laughing, the innocent question suddenly turned a little off color, and the camera quickly moved away from her.

Perhaps the most rumor-like blooper of all was one made by Soupy Sales, the children's television comedian, in January 1965. On a whim one day, he asked all his young viewers to find their parents' wallets and pocketbooks and take out "those little green pieces of paper with pictures of George Washington, Benjamin Franklin, Lincoln, and Jefferson, and send them to me and I'll send you a postcard from Puerto Rico." He received four $1 bills from his fans and a suspension notice from the station. The kids apparently could tell Soupy was joking even if the station executives couldn't. His viewers rallied to his side, signing petitions, calling the station, and picketing. Five days later Soupy was back on the air.

★ ★ Jerry Lewis is considered a comic genius in France, on a par with Charlie Chaplin, Harold Lloyd, and Buster Keaton. (1960s)

True. This is one of the great unsolved mysteries of our time. For some reason the French love Jerry Lewis. Even serious French film critics have dedicated time and energy to his comedy; two publications, *Premier Plan* and *Cinema d'Aujourd'hui,* have devoted entire issues to Lewis's films. Maybe it has something to do with all the wine they drink.

★ ★ Mr. Greenjeans, of the "Captain Kangaroo" television show, is the father of rock musician Frank Zappa. (1968)

Not true. But oh, don't you wish it was! Mr. Greenjeans was (and still is) played by Hugh Brannum, and Frank Zappa's father is named Francis Vincent Zappa, Sr. The two men are entirely unrelated, and by no means the same person.

The Greenjeans-Zappa connection was forged in the public mind by a song on Zappa's "Hot Rats" album, titled "Son of Mr. Green Genes." The song is not autobiographical. Zappa simply liked the play on words.

Moon Unit Zappa *is* Frank Zappa's daughter. She did write (with her father's help) the popular song "Valley Girl," and her parents did give her that name. The other Zappa kids are named Dweezil, Diva, and Ahmet Emuukha Rodan.

Frank Zappa   Hugh Brannum as Mr. Greenjeans

★ ★ Thomas Pynchon and J. D. Salinger are actually the same person. (1960s)

Not true. Both writers guard their privacy zealously, and their absence from the public eye has inevitably led to speculation and rumor.

After a stunning early success—*The Catcher in the Rye* was almost universally acclaimed by critics on its publication in 1951, and has since sold close to 10 million copies—J. D. Salinger dropped abruptly from the literary scene. His last published story appeared in the *New Yorker* in 1964, and since then the author has lived in relative seclusion in his Cornish, New Hampshire home. Readers who loved *The Catcher in the Rye* and Salinger's other writings naturally wonder what he is up to—whether he ever plans to publish another novel. But Salinger isn't talking. He has always refused interviews with the press, and in order to keep reporters at bay has constructed his house so that the only entrance is through a fifty-foot cement tunnel which is reportedly patrolled by dogs. A *Newsweek* correspondent who talked with Salinger for a few minutes in 1974 asked if he was still writing. The author's reply: "Of course I'm still writing."

Some readers thought they had found the answer to the secret writing of J. D. Salinger in the work of Thomas Pynchon, a writer even more guarded about his personal life than Salinger. The first edition of Pynchon's novel, *The Crying of Lot 49,* was published with a solid black box on the jacket where the author photograph should have been. No photograph of him has ever been published, and only his publisher knows where he lives. The Pynchon/Salinger rumor was elaborated on by John Calvin Batchelor in an article for the *Soho Weekly News* in the late seventies, based on arithmetic about ages and publication dates, and stylistic analysis of the two writers' work. We do know that Pynchon was born on Long Island in 1937, and that he graduated from Cornell University in 1958. From 1960 to 1962, while Salinger is known to have been living in New Hampshire, Pynchon worked as a technical writer for the Boeing Aircraft Corporation. After leaving Boeing he lived for a year in Mexico where he wrote his first novel, *V*.

★ ★ Roy Rogers had his horse Trigger stuffed. (1970s)

True. Trigger can now be seen at the Roy Rogers and Dale Evans Museum in Apple Valley, California, mounted in a case with the stuffed dog Bullet, and Dale's horse, Buttermilk. Rogers was very fond of Trigger—the horse was housebroken, could count to twenty-five by stamping his hoof, and could sign an *X* in a hotel register with a pen gripped in his teeth. When the animal died, says Roy, "I just couldn't put the old fellow in the ground."

Rogers and Evans have saved just about everything from their careers—from their first cowboy boots to "Nellybelle," the jeep from the television series. Rogers says the collecting mission began when he visited Will Rogers's ranch, which had been turned into a museum after the actor's death. Recalls Rogers, "It didn't have anything in it. Just a couple of ropes and things. I made up my mind right then that if I ever got anyplace in this business, I was gonna keep everything. Well I sure did."

Trigger is mounted tastefully; the display is in no way shocking or macabre. Roy and Dale do joke about having each other stuffed when the time comes, but we don't really believe they'll do it.

Trigger as he appears today

★ ★ Walt Disney's body has been frozen in a state of suspended animation, to be revived when a cure for his cancer is discovered. (1969)

Not true. Walt Disney died on December 15, 1966, and his body was cremated. His ashes are now at Forest Lawn Memorial Park in Glendale, California. In January 1967, soon after Disney's death, Dr. James Bedford, a psychologist from Glendale, became the first volunteer to have his body frozen in perpetuity, relying on the dim hope that he might someday be revived and restored to health. Bedford's freezing generated a storm of publicity about the budding cryonics movement—the name adopted by the body-freezing advocates—and the news must have become confused with a report of Disney's death to spawn the rumor.

The first printed version of the Disney rumor appeared in *Ici Paris* in 1969, and it was then picked up in English by such tabloids as the *National Tattler*. The Disney Studio denied the rumor each time it appeared in print, but their objections did little to slow the story's spread. In a 1972 letter published by the *Los Angeles Times*, Diane Disney Miller wrote:

> There is absolutely no truth to the rumor that my father, Walt Disney, wished to be frozen. I doubt that my father had ever heard of cryonics. Cremation was his wish, as was the simple family service we observed for him.

That some people are frozen after death is not a rumor. Since 1967 several people have followed Dr. Bedford down the icy path to immortality, though the cryonics movement has suffered some nasty setbacks along the way. The Cryonics Society of New York, one of the first organizations in the field, went out of business in 1975, and the bodies in its care had to be dispersed. But the worst blow came in March 1980, when families of nine bodies maintained by the Cryonics Society of California became suspicious and investigated the crypt where the corpses were stored. They found that the nitrogen coolant supply had run out, leaving all the bodies badly decomposed.

Despite the bad publicity, one independent company, Trans Time, in Berkeley, California, has managed to maintain its cryonic business on a steady footing. The company added a tenth body to its collection in 1981, and it manages to earn enough on the required $60,000 deposits to keep the corpses frozen indefinitely.

The Walt Disney rumor was not the last to come out of the cryonics movement. Dr. Bedford, the first man to be frozen, was rumored to have thawed in 1974. (He did not.) All high Soviet officials are said to go into the deep freeze after death. And members of the Ringling family—the circus people—are falsely said to be frozen and stored together when they die.

★ ★ A woman in New York won $800,000 in a malpractice suit against her plastic surgeon because he moved her belly button off center during an operation to tighten her stomach. (1979)

True. In 1979 a forty-two-year-old Poughkeepsie woman was awarded $854,000 in State Supreme Court in Manhattan. The woman claimed her plastic surgeon had moved her belly button two and a half inches off center during the operation. The doctor had argued that it was only half an inch off, which he said was "not cosmetically unacceptable." The jury disagreed and was apparently moved by the plaintiff's claim that the operation had left "a large deformed hole" in her stomach and had disrupted her business and her life. Her belly button had been put back where it belonged a year after the ill-fated procedure by another plastic surgeon, who testified on the woman's behalf in the malpractice case. Apparently afraid that her good fortune might not survive an appeal, the woman later settled with the doctor for $200,000.

Another rumor has it that a woman was awarded a fortune in a suit against her doctor who left her with *no* belly button after surgery. We haven't been able to find out whether this really did happen or whether it's just a distortion of the Poughkeepsie woman's story, and heaven knows she'd been distorted enough as it was.

★ ★ John Howard Griffin, author of the book *Black Like Me,* died of skin cancer caused by the chemical he used to change his skin color from white to black. (1960s)

Not true. This rumor started while Griffin was still alive, in fact, while he was traveling extensively to encourage a dialogue between white and black communities across the country. Since many people deeply resented Griffin's book and the racial tensions it exposed—he and his family moved to Mexico for a time after he was hanged in effigy in his hometown of Mansfield, Texas—the rumor has an element of the sinister to it, a satisfied wish for revenge. Since many people who told the story had no quarrel with Griffin or his discoveries, the rumor doubled as a sort of ironic tragedy, showing that those who do good are not exempt from life's cruelties.

Griffin did lead a difficult life. He was blind for eleven years from an injury he suffered in World War II, and, toward the end of his life, he had a leg amputated. But none of his medical misfortunes stemmed from the 1959 skin-darkening treatment. He died in 1980 from complications caused by diabetes.

Another racial rumor, twisted the other way, holds that Dr. Charles Drew, a black doctor whose research helped in the establishment of blood banks, bled to death when he was refused care at a whites-only hospital in 1950. This story is equally false. Dr. Drew, who did important research on the use of blood plasma for transfusions, was driving a car through North Carolina with three other black doctors, en route to Tuskeegee University in Alabama, when in the early hours of the morning of April 1, 1950, he fell asleep at the wheel and drove off the road. As the car went out of control, it threw Drew out and rolled over him, nearly severing his leg and badly injuring his head. All four doctors were taken by ambulance to Alamance General Hospital, where they received prompt medical care. Dr. Drew died in the emergency room after two hours of treatment. Dr. John Ford, one of Drew's companions in the car, was admitted to the hospital and treated for several days. He later wrote to the hospital to say the care he received had been satisfactory.

A story about a doctor who died from an affliction he helped to control turns out to be true. Dr. Howard Taylor Ricketts, who isolated the bacteria that causes typhus and identified the insect that transmits it, died from the disease only weeks after his discovery in 1910. Ricketts was portrayed by Errol Flynn in the 1937 film *Green Light*.

═══════════════════════════════

★ ★ John F. Kennedy is alive and in a coma in a Houston hospital. (1964)

Not true. According to this rumor, the shots in Dallas hit Kennedy in the head, but did not kill him. As there was no provision in the Constitution for the removal from office of a brain-damaged president, Lyndon Johnson, with the help of the CIA and the FBI, announced Kennedy's death while transferring him to a top-secret wing of a Houston hospital. Since then, the rumor has placed him in mysterious facilities in Alaska and the Swiss Alps and even at the Onassis mansion in Greece, where, the story goes, Jackie has had special

103

wheelchair ramps installed so that he can move himself around. Pathetic, but not true.

This is the most widespread of a group of rumors about public personalities who have supposedly survived their announced deaths. Most are figures who died suddenly at the height of their careers, and the stories probably express a longing for their return and an unwillingness to accept the reality of their deaths.

James Dean, the movie actor, was rumored to have survived his 1955 car accident and ended up as a human vegetable in an Indiana hospital. Jim Morrison, the mythic leader of the sixties rock group the Doors, is reputed to be lingering in a coma in a hospital in France. This rumor started in direct response to the guarded announcements that followed Morrison's death in 1971. The first reports came almost a week after the twenty-five-year-old rock star was found dead in the bathroom of his Paris hotel room, and two days after he had been secretly buried in a Paris cemetery. A spokesman from Morrison's public relations agency told the press only that the singer had died of "natural causes." There had been no funeral service and no autopsy. Morrison's manager, Bill Siddons, later described the burial as a very private affair, attended only by himself, Morrison's wife Pamela, and three friends. "We just threw some flowers and dirt and said goodbye."

In the week before the announcement, rumors of Morrison's death circulated in Paris and London. Reporters who checked them out by calling the Paris hotel were told the singer was "not dead but very tired and resting in a hospital." After the death was announced, the rumors flip-flopped, focussing on those interim reports of his survival. He was rumored to be still resting in the unnamed Paris hospital, or, later, to be living in Africa, either as a revolutionary leader or a poet. We have even heard that he is back in the rock music business, performing now as Ace Feeley of the group Kiss.

A more recent rumor has brought Elvis Presley back to life, and, unlike the other survivors, Presley is rumored to be in good health. The most common version of the story claims that he will be resurrected in 1984 with a dramatic re-entry to the music scene. Others claim that Elvis started making public appearances in 1983, playing Eddie Rabbit songs in Hawaiian nightclubs or performing in European bars. All these stories are of course untrue. Presley died in 1977, and thirty thousand of his fans filed past his body as it lay in state at Graceland, his Memphis mansion. The rumors of his survival have been encouraged by some of the less scrupulous tabloids, one of which went to the unfortunate extreme of calling for his body to be exhumed.

The actual secretive escape and survival of many top Nazi officials after World War II has fueled false rumors about the survival of others who are known to have died—foremost among them Adolf Hitler. Hitler's body was found and examined by the Russian forces that conquered Berlin in May 1945. Though badly charred by an attempt at cremation, it was identifiable by its dental work. But for some reason, the Russian autopsy reports and photographs of the body were sent to Moscow and quietly filed away. To further confuse the issue, Stalin and other official Soviet spokesmen began to propound the line that Hitler had escaped alive, probably by air, and was living in Spain or South America under the protection of a fascist government.

Western investigators had to rely on the testimony of eyewitnesses to the cremation—guards and government ministers who were with Hitler in the last days of the war—to prove that he had indeed died. Historians writing in the years just after World War II were forced to admit that though they knew Hitler to be dead, they had no evidence to show that his body had ever been found.

In the years since 1945, that evidence has been slowly forthcoming. Some key witnesses who had disappeared after the war have been released from Soviet prisons—one of the dentists who identified Hitler's teeth was released in 1954, followed in 1956 by a guard who helped bury the body and who led Russian investigators to the grave. Finally, in 1968, an allegedly complete account of the Russian discoveries was published in Lev Bezymenski's *The Death of Adolf Hitler,* complete with a photograph of the body and the full text of the autopsy report. The location of the body itself has still not been revealed by the Russians.

In spite of all the evidence to the contrary, the rumor of Hitler's survival endures, a tribute to the power of a few words from the mouth of Joseph Stalin. But the myth can't last forever. Hitler may be alive in the rumor, but he's getting old—he'd be ninety-five in 1984.

★ ★ Marilyn Monroe was killed by the CIA because she knew too much about the plot to assassinate President Kennedy. (1964)

Not true. Because Marilyn Monroe's death occurred roughly a year before Kennedy's assassination, and because both deaths gave rise to a number of rumors, it was probably inevitable that the two sets of rumors would merge.

Even before Kennedy was shot, stories were circulating that Monroe had not committed suicide, as officially reported, but had been murdered. Some of her fans apparently could not accept the fact that she had killed herself after achieving such success as an actress. One of the rumors claimed that the mafia had done her in because she had embarrassed Joe DiMaggio by not settling down with him. (DiMaggio and Monroe were married for less than a year in 1954, and in the months before Monroe's death some speculated that the two might remarry.) Rumors also circulated about her reported trysts with an assortment of notables, including the president and Robert Kennedy, and even Albert Einstein. From the rumor of her liaison with Robert Kennedy grew another rumor: that he had told her some things she shouldn't have heard—secrets about the investigation of Jimmy Hoffa, and about CIA plots in Cuba—and that she was murdered to keep this information quiet.

The assassination of President Kennedy in November 1963 stunned the nation, probably more completely than any other tragedy in a generation. Lee Harvey Oswald seemed too minor a character to have committed such a world-shaking act alone, so rumors began to fill the gap. Based on the slimmest evidence—the time between the shots on a poor-quality tape recording, and the posture of the passengers in the president's limousine as seen on an eight-millimeter home-movie filmstrip—a second gunman was discussed, then a wider conspiracy involving at first the Cuban government, and then the FBI and the CIA, and even Lyndon Johnson—as he was the man who benefited most immediately from the death. When Oswald was shot, the man the nation saw die on television was explained away by the rumors as merely a double—the real Oswald had been spirited safely to Russia.

The Cuban connection in the assassination gained renewed credibility when it was revealed in 1976 that in the early 1960s, the CIA had very definitely been behind several plots to assassinate Fidel Castro (and behind other strange schemes, including one to create a drought in Cuba by seeding rain clouds so that they would empty before reaching the island—plots that would sound like bizarre rumors had they not been admitted by the CIA). Wasn't it reasonable to suspect that Castro might try to retaliate by having Kennedy killed?

Marilyn Monroe came into the assassination rumors when it was remembered that she had been friendly with the president—too friendly, according to the whispers. From there it was but a small leap of the paranoid imagination to surmise that she had found out about the assassination before her death. (Had the President told her? Or Robert Kennedy? And if they knew, why did they let it happen?) She diligently wrote everything she heard in her mysterious red diary, which somehow disappeared from her other belongings in the coroner's safe, so the story goes. The diary has been seen in dozens of places around the world, and most of those who claim to have read it say that it gives the lowdown on the Kennedy assassination, but no one has managed to keep it long enough to offer it for public scrutiny. More recent rumors have placed Monroe in a secret government hospital under heavy sedation; it has even been suggested that she escaped from the hospital and is living under an alias.

Conspiracy rumors seem to be an inevitable outgrowth of an assassination. After the death of Abraham Lincoln, which *was* planned by a small group of plotters, the web of conspiracy was imagined to reach all the way to the leaders of the just-defeated Confederacy. (The murder occurred only five days after the South's surrender.) Many southern leaders, including Jefferson Davis, were actually arrested in connection with the assassination, though they were later released without trial. Years later, the rumor boomeranged and blamed Lincoln's own secretary of war, Edward L. Stanton, as the shadowy figure behind the plot, mostly because of his zealous direction of the prosecution and hanging of the actual conspirators. It was thought that by quickly putting them out of the way he was keeping evidence from coming out about his own involvement in the scheme. This theory has little historical basis.

After Martin Luther King's assassination in 1968, James Earl Ray testified that he had been aided in the killing by a mysterious man, known to him only as Raoul. That testimony, though never supported by any evidence, started rumors about a conspiracy behind King's murder as well. Rumors have even named Raoul as the second gunman in the Kennedy assassination.

It seems that we need to believe in a conspiracy when faced with the murder of a great man by a lone and probably crazed killer. Such a death puts a trivial end to a noble life. The conspiracy rumors may be an attempt to embellish history by inventing a murder of grander and more appropriate proportions.

★ ★ Military Intelligence agents regularly visit video arcades and take down the initials of high scorers. The information is stored on Pentagon computers for future use. (1981)

Not true. Mastery of video games may give some indication of qualities like good eye-hand coordination, quick reaction time, and presence of mind under pressure. But it also indicates the amount of practice a player has had on a particular game. If the Air Force wanted to use video games to select candidates for pilot training, it would most likely test all subjects on a new game that none had tried before.

The rumor is pure video-arcade fantasy—an asteroid zapper's dream. What, we wonder, would the Pentagon do with a computerful of high-scorers' initials? Ask draftees whose initials match if they were the same "CGW" who scored eight million playing Space Invaders on June 2, 1981, in an arcade on Route 1 in Saugus, Massachusetts? And if the answer were yes would that mean a transfer to astronaut training? Or would agents track the mysterious "CGW" down immediately and offer a prime spot in an officer-training program?

It must make for some pleasant wishful thinking, but it's just too farfetched. All the same, it wouldn't hurt to play those buttons extra carefully if you spotted a man with black tie shoes snooping around the arcade, would it? He might just be the owner, but then again . . .

★ ★ Jack the Ripper was a member of the British royal family, and, rather than reveal his identity, police pretended that the case was never solved. (1970)

Not true. Jack the Ripper murdered five prostitutes in London's East End between August and November 1888 and left behind just enough clues to keep criminologists puzzling for decades. Police at the time suspected that a doctor had done the killings, as the bodies had been partially dissected. At the top of their list of suspects were a Dr. Ostrog, described as a "mad Russian doctor," and a Dr. M. J. Druitt, who drowned himself in January 1889. Other theories at the time blamed the murder on a mysterious Dr. Stanley, who escaped to South America, on a Polish Jew named Kominski, on a butcher from a nearby slaughterhouse, and on an unidentified midwife, who, as a woman, avoided suspicion for the crimes. Sir Arthur Conan Doyle favored this last explanation.

Since then theorists have focused on the account of a witness who saw a "well-dressed" man talking to the last victim shortly before her death. They have hung on that frail thread of evidence the most elaborate theories, the most remarkable of which was published by Dr. T. E. A. Stowells, who in 1970 concluded that the Ripper had been Edward, Duke of Clarence, the grandson of Queen Victoria and heir to the throne of England. Stowell theorized that Edward's death in 1892, officially attributed to influenza, was actually caused by softening of the brain due to syphilis. His declining mental state, according to Stowell, had caused him to commit the murders. The story received wide publicity, mostly in the form of articles questioning its plausibility, and word of mouth has since embedded the theory as fact in the public imagination. Other researchers have shown quite conclusively that the actual events don't fit the theory, but it seems that the rumor, once started, is not going to be stopped by mere truth.

A more recent explanation for the murders has pinned them on the duke's close friend and tutor, J. K. Stephen, who also died in 1892, apparently of the affliction that had caused him mental troubles since 1885. We grant that this theory is possible, but, after nearly a hundred years, so much of the evidence has vanished that there can be no way of proving anything with certainty. What keeps the "Ripperologists" (as the speculators call themselves) going is the hope that some proof will come from the secret Scotland Yard file on the case, which will finally be made public in 1992.

★ ★ Occidental Petroleum mogul Armand Hammer was named by his father for the official symbol of the Socialist Labor Party—a worker's arm holding a hammer.

Unverifiable. Armand Hammer's father, Julius Hammer, was one of the founding members of the American Communist Party, and, according to socialist Bertram Wolfe, he named his son in honor of socialism. Armand Hammer has consistently denied this and claims that he was named for a character in Alexander Dumas's novel *La Dame aux Camelias*.

★ ★ Amelia Earhart was on a secret mission to photograph the Japanese military buildup in the Pacific when she disappeared in 1937. She was captured by the Japanese and may still be alive. (1937)

Unsubstantiated. Amelia Earhart disappeared over the Pacific on July 2, 1937, while on the last leg of her much-publicized around-the-world flight, which was to have ended the next day in California. She and her navigator, Fred Noonan, took off from Lae, New Guinea, heading for Howland Island, a tiny coral outcrop 2,556 miles to the northeast, where they planned to refuel and head on to Hawaii. They never arrived, though they came close enough to start up radio contact with the Coast Guard cutter *Itasca,* stationed at the island to aid the two fliers in any emergency. Most of the experts who have studied the records of the radio broadcasts during the flight conclude that the plane missed Howland Island and went down in the vast stretch of empty ocean just to the north. Boats searching the area that day reported rough seas, which would have broken the plane up very quickly.

But the reconnaissance/survival story is not easily put to rest. No one *really* knows where Earhart was during most of that last flight. It is true that the United States government suspected the Japanese of fortifying the Marshall Islands, which lay to the north of the flier's planned route, and which were sealed off from foreign observation by patrolling Japanese boats. Earhart was an acquaintance of Eleanor Roosevelt, and had met and spoken with the president on several occasions. Believers in her survival assume the president gave her secret orders at one of these meetings, but in fact there is no way of knowing what they discussed.

Hollywood first promoted the spy angle in the 1943 film *Flight for Freedom*—based roughly on the Amelia Earhart story—which portrayed the aviatrix deliberately crashing near a Japanese island, so that U.S. ships would search the area and observe the Japanese installations under the pretense of trying to find the downed plane. Earhart's mother gave the spy-theorists another big boost in a widely circulated 1949 interview: "Amelia told me many things. But there were some things she didn't tell me. I am convinced she was on some sort of government mission, probably on verbal orders."

As to what became of the flier, we have our choice of dozens of eyewitness reports putting her on islands all over the Pacific and in Japan, alive in grass huts or in wartime prisons, or executed by the Japanese. Two Amelia Earhart enthusiasts claim to have located her in New Jersey, where she refuses to cooperate and admit her identity. (Her husband has threatened to call the police if the two don't end their pestering.)

The U.S. Navy searched the area around Howland Island until July 18, 1937, when it gave the two fliers up for dead and recalled the assigned ships and planes. Amelia Earhart was declared legally dead on January 5, 1939.

Others, too, live on in the public imagination in that gray region of possible survivors. Anastasia, the youngest daughter of Tsar Nicholas II of Russia and the greatgranddaughter of Britain's Queen Victoria, may have escaped the 1918 execution of the Russian royal family. Since 1920, when she was rescued from a suicide attempt in Berlin, Anna Anderson (now Anastasia Manahan, a resident of Virginia), has quietly maintained that she is Anastasia. Many support her position, including servants and friends of the Romanov family who knew Anastasia in Russia. But over the course of more than sixty years she has been unable to win the recognition of the Tsar's closest relatives, his royal relations in Germany, Denmark, and England. Unfortunately, no fingerprints exist of the young grand duchess, so proof of her identiy will never be conclusive. But handwriting experts have consistently found her writing to match the young Anastasia's. If she is an imposter she is an astoundingly good one, for her knowledge of obscure details about the life of the Russian royal family is immense. If she is Anastasia, then her rejection by her royal relatives is tragic.

John Dillinger, the famous bank robber, is believed by many to have escaped to Mexico in 1934. Adherents to this theory claim that the man shot down outside a Chicago theater on July 22, 1934 was an innocent victim who resembled Dillinger but lacked the criminal's known scars and wounds. This is not born out by the facts. Dillinger underwent plastic surgery for the removal of his fingerprints and several moles and scars on his face just two months before his death, and as a result some people who had known him thought the body looked like a different man. His family identified the body positively, but their assertions seemed only to make the disbelievers more adamant. His father, worried that someone might dig the body up to make sure, had the grave sealed with scrap iron and cement.

"Butch" Cassidy is claimed by some to have escaped from his reported ambush by Bolivian soldiers in 1908 and to have lived until 1937 in Johnnie, Nevada, under an alias. And Martin Bormann, Hitler's private secretary, probably did escape from the Fuhrer-bunker on May 1, 1945, when Russian forces moved into Berlin. He disappeared completely, and many believe that he is now living comfortably in Argentina.

★ ★ Albert Einstein's brain now sits in a cider box in the corner of a doctor's office in Wichita, Kansas. (1978)

True. Or at least that's where the brain was when Steven Levy, a reporter from *New Jersey Monthly* magazine, tracked it down in 1978. Einstein had requested that, after his death, his brain be used for research. When he died on April 18, 1955, the most celebrated brain of our time was carefully removed from Einstein's body and preserved. The rest of the body was cremated.

The brain fell under the care of Dr. Thomas S. Harvey, the pathologist at the Princeton, New Jersey, hospital where Einstein had died. Dr. Harvey made plans for a team of experts to study the brain to try to unlock the mystery of its genius. But after his first examination of the tissue he commented: "It looks just like anybody else's."

Microscopic sections were taken and distributed for closer study, but, when the New Jersey reporter tracked down Dr. Harvey in 1978, no findings had been published. Dr. Harvey, by then a supervisor at a biological testing laboratory in Wichita, offered to show the reporter the pieces of the brain that remained. The reporter was spellbound as the doctor reached into a cardboard cider box in the corner of his office and pulled out a Mason jar holding the specimen:

> I had risen to look into the jar, but now I was sunk in my chair, speechless. My eyes were fixed upon that jar as I tried to comprehend that these pieces of gunk bobbing up and down had caused a revolution in physics and quite possibly changed the course of civilization. *There it was!*

Dr. Harvey and the brain have since moved on to Weston, Missouri, where the doctor has plans to at last publish the results of his twenty-nine-year study. His findings? The brain is not unusual in any way.

★ ★ A UFO crashed during the Eisenhower administration, and the bodies of the occupants are on ice at Wright-Patterson Air Force Base in Ohio. (1955)

Unsubstantiated. The entire field of UFO research is clouded by rumor and speculation and hampered by lack of hard evidence. Frustrated by their inability to find any fragments of spaceships or any space beings, many UFO researchers accuse the U.S. government of hoarding all such evidence. The charges against the government do not explain how it has managed to snatch up every space object to hit the earth before anyone else could get a look. Do flying saucers only crash in North America?

Part of the suspicion of the U.S. government—and such suspicion has grown up around the world, not just in this country—stems from the secretive way it has conducted its investigations of the subject. The Air Force and the CIA openly monitored UFO reports during the years after World War II, thinking that some of the sightings might involve Russian aircraft. In 1952, after they'd found most of the reports to be spurious, the two agencies closed their books— or so they said. Both the Air Force and the CIA actually continued their investigations in secret, though their goal has remained the detection of Russian planes.

Out of the secrecy and suspicion has grown a host of rumors. The Air Force is said to have retrieved a UFO from northern Mexico in 1948 and obtained from it the technological breakthroughs necessary to launch the space program. Another spacecraft allegedly crashed near Kingman, Arizona, in 1953, and a retired Air Force colonel now claims to have seen the dead aliens at the site—they were about four feet tall and had silverish complexions.

A more involved rumor tells of a meeting between President Eisenhower and a group of aliens in February 1954. According to the story, five spaceships landed at Edwards Air Force Base in California, and President Eisenhower was hurriedly summoned from his vacation retreat in nearby Palm Springs to meet with the aliens. The *National Enquirer* reported the tale in an October 1982 article headlined "Ike Met Space Aliens." The newspaper based much of its article on the testimony of "a former top U.S. test pilot," who described the aliens demonstrating their remarkably sophisticated crafts to the humans, and speaking with the president in English. Eisenhower asked them to leave quietly so as not to create panic on earth.

Rumors of other encounters include the crash of a cigar-shaped spacecraft in Aurora, Texas, on April 19, 1897, and of a flying saucer in New Mexico in 1962. In the first incident the spacecraft is said to have smashed into Judge J. S. Proctor's house. As reported by S. E. Hayden in the Dallas and Fort Worth newspapers the next day, the pilot was mutilated in the crash, but "enough remains were picked up to determine it was not an inhabitant of this world. The men of the community gathered it up, and it was given a Christian burial at the Aurora cemetery." The local cemetery commission must still keep a watchful eye on the cemetery to thwart the repeated attempts at vandalism by UFO enthusiasts hoping to find the alien's body. After the 1962 crash, the bodies of two aliens are said to have been recovered and examined by researchers at an East Coast hospital.

There *are* records of some mysterious and unexplained sightings that might possibly have been encounters with alien spaceships, but these tales of meetings and discovery of bodies are not among them. All the encounters we have described fall into the category of rumor and are almost certainly the product of fertile imaginations.

★ ★ Former president Jimmy Carter sighted a UFO while he was Governor of Georgia and reported it to UFO researchers. (1977)

True. Carter casually mentioned the sighting while attending a southern governors' conference in 1973. Several southern newspapers picked the story up, quoting him as saying, "I don't laugh at people any more when they say they've seen UFO's, because I've seen one myself." Two UFO organizations responded by sending Carter sighting-report forms, which he filled out and returned.

According to his reports, Carter spotted the object in the sky while standing with about ten other men outside the Lions' Club of Leary, Georgia, in October 1969. Carter was there to give a dinner speech. All the men saw the object, and they watched it for ten or twelve minutes before it disappeared. Carter described the object as "bluish at first, then reddish." It changed in size from that of a "planet" to the "apparent size of the moon," and became "at one time as bright as the moon." Carter wrote that "it seemed to move toward us from a distance, stopped and moved partially away. It returned, then departed. It came close . . . maybe 300 to 1000 yards . . . moved away, came close and then moved away."

Carter was almost surely describing the planet Venus, then in its brightest phase and probably distorted that night by atmospheric conditions. Many people mistake bright planets for UFOs. One seasoned Air Force pilot went into evasive maneuvers one night to avoid hitting a UFO—which, upon investigation, turned out to have been the moon.

★ ★ No astronauts ever went to the moon. The televised landings were staged at a secret government base in Nevada. (1968)

Not true. An astonishing number of people believed this, and many still hold to their conviction. Apparently the momentous event was more than some people could absorb as fact. The landings also came at a time when the public was extremely suspicious of the government's conduct of the war in Vietnam, and some were ready to doubt any official announcement.

The 1978 film *Capricorn One* tried to cash in on this rumor. The film stars James Brolin, Sam Waterston, and O. J. Simpson as three astronauts acting out the hoodwinking of the century in the Nevada desert.

This rumor must represent some sort of pinnacle of cynical disbelief. Instead of accepting the news and taking pride in a tremendous human accomplishment, believers of the staged-landing story view the moon landings as cause for scorn and mistrust. We prefer our cynicism in smaller doses. Astronauts *did* go to the moon, and they left moon rovers, flags, footprints, and trash up there to prove it.

═══════════════════════════════════════

★ ★ A fleet of dead cosmonauts is orbiting the earth, casualties of repeated accidents in the Russian space program. (1961)

Not true. Rumors of fatal Soviet rocket failures began to make the rounds almost as soon as the successful Sputnik launch was announced in 1957. The stories went so far as to name the dead cosmonauts and give precise dates for their failed missions—Alexei Ledowski in 1957, Serenty Schiborin in 1958, and even a woman, Mirija Gromov, in 1959. By the time Yuriy Gagarin made his historic flight in April 1961, becoming the first man to orbit the earth, the rumors had accounted for at least a dozen grisly fatalities—astronauts trapped in orbit, roasted alive when their spaceships malfunctioned, or blown to bits on the launching pad. Even Gagarin was rumored to be a stand-in for a dead pilot.

Because the official reports from the Soviet space program were less than complete and often contradictory, it is easy to see how the rumors started. Failed missions were described only vaguely in the Soviet press, while the successes were lavished with patriotic detail. And because the Russians were trouncing the United States so dramatically in the space race, many Americans were ready to believe anything they heard about Soviet disasters.

The rumors were helped along by a western press that for several years adopted a decidedly casual standard of reporting when dealing with the Soviet space program. The cosmonaut deaths made the pages of *Time, Newsweek, U.S. News and World Report,* and *Reader's Digest* in reports based on the shakiest of evidence.

In fact, there were probably *no* in-flight fatalities during the early years of the Russian space program. In a report for the U.S. House of Representatives Subcommittee on Space Science, scholars of the Soviet space program who work at the Library of Congress analyzed these rumors and found them without foundation. As they put it,

We are asked by those who believe many Russians have died in orbit in effect to accept the existence of a second Soviet manned flight program run with reckless abandon which often kills the flight crews. These purported failure flights . . . apparently would be conducted without advance warning, . . . and use different models of larger, untried ships which always kill their crews or leave them stranded in orbit. Yet the "flights" cannot be detected by the same U.S. tracking systems that usually find even chance pieces of space debris at the altitudes manned flights occur. This is hardly credible.

★ ★ The oil companies have developed an inexpensive pill that allows cars to travel a hundred miles on a gallon of ordinary gasoline, but they are keeping it off the market in order to sustain current levels of gasoline sales. (1974)

Not true. This rumor has its origins in hoaxes and investment scams that go back to the nineteenth century. In 1874 John E. W. Keely first demonstrated his hydro-pneumatic-pulsating vacue machine, which he claimed could drive a thirty-car train from New York to Philadelphia at a speed of sixty miles per hour, using just one quart of water for fuel. The machine still needed some refinements, of course, but Keely was able to raise thousands of dollars from investors so that he could complete his invention. He never did perfect the machine, and he continued to swindle money for the rest of his life by pretending to work on the contraption.

In the thirties, con men came up with the "gasoline pills" as a way to raise easy cash. A man would pull into a gas station and ask the attendant to fill his car's gas tank up with water. Then he would drop a pill into the tank, explaining that it converted the water into gasoline. If the attendant seemed properly intrigued, the man would sell him several pills for all the cash he had in the station. The pills, of course, did nothing; the water had been diverted from the actual gas tank, and the con man left with a wad of cash.

Magical gasoline pills came back as rumors during the oil shortages of the seventies—along with carburetors that could burn water and experimental cars that could travel a thousand miles on a tank of gas. This last rumor is often told in a more intricate version: a car dealer sold a woman an experimental car by mistake. The vehicle could travel a thousand miles on a gallon of gasoline, and the manufacturer didn't want people to know about it. When the woman brought it back for its first routine servicing, the dealer offered her $30,000 if she would accept a substitute car and keep the matter quiet.

A related rumor tells of a forever-burning lightbulb developed by a major electric appliance firm. Once the discovery was made, company executives realized that if they sold the bulbs they would be putting themselves out of business, so they suppressed the invention. Or, a variant rumor holds, they concealed the invention because they are in collusion with the electric power companies.

These gas-pill and forever-burning-lightbulb rumors have something in common with the car-for-a-penny rumors that circulated earlier. In each, a simple, cheap item makes a revolutionary positive change in our lives. But the new versions have added a heavy dose of cynicism and paranoia to the innocent old rumors: they tell us that we may never get our hands on the wonderful inventions because of the powerful machinations of huge corporations.

As feelings of suspicion and resentment were directed most strongly at the large oil companies in the mid-seventies—they did record huge profits in the years of shortage while the rest of us suffered—it is not surprising that the most vicious rumors were directed against them. They were rumored to have conspired in creating the shortage by withholding oil from the market or by not operating their refineries to their full capacity. The most elaborate story told of intentional dumping. According to the rumor, a newsman followed a gasoline truck down a remote country road and filmed it as the driver got out and dumped its full load of gas into the dirt. His film clearly shows the identification on the truck of a major oil company. The rumor ends with the punch line that "60 Minutes" has obtained the footage and they will soon air it as part of an exposé.

Such rumors died down as soon as oil supplies became more plentiful. But chances are they will dust themselves off and reappear when people again become frustrated over the cost of gasoline and again need to consider the rising rates the work of villainous oil companies.

★ ★ Some of the major tobacco companies own marijuana fields in Mexico and, in anticipation of the legalization of the drug, have already chosen brand names and designed packages. (1960s)

Not true. There is no factual basis for this rumor, according to experts at NORMAL, the Washington-based lobby group that is working to legalize marijuana. They explain that climatic conditions in the United States are actually better suited for the cultivation of marijuana than those in the hotter countries south of the border. And, since the tobacco companies already own fertile farmland in the southern states, they have no need to spend money on foreign real estate.

As for the brand names, it is possible, though unlikely, that some of the tobacco companies have planned that far into marijuana's uncertain future. But, even if some of the companies have gone so far as to choose brand names, they almost certainly wouldn't have picked the names mentioned in the rumors—"Panama Red," "Acapulco Gold," and other common marijuana "street" names. Consider the subtlety of cigarette names—like "Camel," "True," "Winston," and "Vantage"—and you will realize that we have come to expect a more creative effort than "Virginia Tan."

Some versions of the rumor go even further to claim that the chosen brand names have already been given trademark protection. This cannot be true. Trademark protection is only available to products after they have been put on the market. So you won't see any trademarked marijuana cigarette brands until some time after the drug is legalized, if indeed it ever is.

Though the rumors about Mexican land purchases and trademarked brand names are farfetched, we do know that the tobacco companies are interested in marijuana and that the facilities they use to manufacture ordinary cigarettes can also be used to manufacture marijuana cigarettes. When a government-sanctioned research project requires a supply of such cigarettes, the tobacco companies are hired to do the rolling. And, because they have the manufacturing facilities, the companies would be risking the loss of a competitive edge in a huge potential market if they allowed a change in the marijuana laws to catch them unprepared. That they are not about to let that happen is evident by another clue. At press conferences the tobacco companies often supply newsmen with lists of questions that their spokesmen are prepared to answer. Those questions regularly include a few about marijuana.

★ ★ MIT and Stanford University students have developed a "black box" that enables them to make free telephone calls around the world. (1960s)

True. During the 1960s some students at those universities did develop devices that enabled them to bypass the telephone company's billing system. The "black box" was one of the first and one of the simplest. It worked on incoming calls by continuing the telephone's ringing after the receiver had been picked up—fooling the phone system into thinking the call had not been answered. With the bell turned down to its lowest setting, the two parties could talk quite comfortably for as long as they wished, and the caller would never be billed.

A more complex device was the "blue box," which worked by emitting a perfect 26,000-cycle tone, electronically erasing the billing connection to the calling telephone once access had been gained to the long-distance trunk lines. With the call then in the long-distance circuits, it could be rerouted wherever the caller pleased—for a free call to any phone in the world. If discovered, such calls could be traced, so they were usually made from pay phone to pay phone. Some very successful figures in the field of computers admit to having dabbled in blue boxes during their college years—among them Stephen Jobs, the twenty-eight-year-old founder and president of Apple Computer.

The "red box" worked on a more basic concept, and from pay telephones only. It duplicated the tones made by various coins as they were dropped into the phone, freeing the caller from carrying any change. Rumor had it that a talented flute player could do the same thing.

The aim of the various box designers was to refine their devices into smaller and smaller formats. The first blue boxes were the size of a toaster oven—completely impractical for phone-booth use. But by the mid-seventies, underground engineers turned out compact models that could fit into a cigarette package.

While most of the telephone bandits worked with sophisticated computer technology, the most famous among them were two men who used the simplest of tools. Joe ("the Whistler") Engressia had such perfect pitch that he could whistle the 26,000-cycle tone used by the blue boxes. Box builders used to call him to tune their machines. And John ("the Captain") Draper started his free-call career with a plastic whistle from a box of Cap'n Crunch cereal that happened to emit the blue-box tone. Both men spent time in jail for their adventures, the Whistler after a lengthy chat with a guard at the American Embassy in Moscow. Engressia later made good by ferreting out problems in the telephone system and volunteering suggestions for improvement to A. T. & T. In 1977 Mountain Bell hired him as a problem analyst. The Captain worked for a while as a telecommunications consultant. He now heads his own computer software company.

★ ★ Welch's candy company is owned by the founder of the John Birch Society. (1960s)

Not true. But Robert Welch, the founder of the John Birch Society, *was* at one time a partner in the company that made Welch's Junior Mints—those little chocolate-covered mints that we always buy at the movies. In fact, Welch invented the candy and its name. He left the company in 1952 in order to pursue his anti-Communist activities full time; the company remained in the care of his brother. So Welch never actually had any connection to the company while he was running the John Birch Society. Did we hear a sigh of relief from all our liberal Junior Mint-loving readers? You can rest easier knowing you never directly supported the wrong cause.

That same Robert Welch was solidly behind all the rumors we heard about fluoridation of public drinking water—that it was a Communist plot; that once the mechanisms were in place for adding fluoride, saboteurs could easily add poison or LSD during a Communist attack; and that fluoridation would lead straight to socialized medicine. When the idea of fluoridation of drinking water was first proposed in the thirties as an inexpensive and effective way to reduce the incidence of tooth decay in children, it seemed like a sensible and beneficial move. Studies showed that in communities with naturally high levels of fluoride in the water, children had much better teeth. And the first communities to add fluoride to their water started to see immediate and positive results. But in the early fifties a very vocal opposition sprang up.

In 1951, the city of Seattle decided to consider fluoridation after examining a study done by the city's PTA that showed clear and beneficial results in other communities that had tried it. The city council held public meetings on the proposal, which generated only favorable discussion. It looked like fluoridation was a sure winner. Then the city's Christian Scientists organized themselves to fight the measure, which they saw as an attempt at forced medication. Hot on their heels came two secular anti-fluoridation groups, the Washington State Council Against Fluoridation and the National Nutrition League. The battle intensified, and the charges against fluoridation multiplied. It was labeled human experimentation with shades of Nazi Germany. Pamphlets were distributed that linked fluorides with hardening of the arteries, loss of memory, "cavities in head bones, . . . undue financial anxiety, . . . and nymphomania." As the movement against fluoridation gathered momentum nationwide, the Communist-plot charges entered the picture, along with rumors that fluoridation was a plot by the aluminum industry to get rid of its chemical wastes (fluorides *are* used in refining aluminum, but the supplies for use in drinking water come mostly from the chemical fertilizer industry), or that it was a plot by the sugar interests—with fluorides in the water, it was thought mothers would allow their children to eat more candy.

Throughout the fifties and early sixties, the dispute continued at a highly emotional pitch. Representatives of the anti-fluoridation forces who came to Washington to testify before a Senate committee on the subject in 1956 brought "natural" water with them to avoid drinking the city's fluoridated water, and they refused to bathe during their stay. But the interest of children's teeth gradually began to win the upper hand, and, as more and more communities began to add fluorides to their water without any detectable negative side-effects, the controversy began to die. Today fluoridation is largely a non-issue.

Those of you who heard that John Wayne was the head of the John Birch Society in Orange County, California, in the sixties heard wrong. This was a popular rumor that probably grew out of Wayne's right-wing political leanings. Wayne was never a member of the John Birch Society. But he was no liberal, either. Wayne backed Senator Joseph McCarthy for president in the 1952 Republican primary. He backed Richard Nixon in the forties when Nixon ran for Congress as an anti-Red crusader. Wayne was also involved in the formation of the Motion Picture Alliance for the Preservation of American Ideals, a group that aided in the blacklisting of actors suspected of Communist beliefs. And George Wallace, by some accounts, considered Wayne for his running mate in the 1968 presidential race. Wouldn't that have been a team?

★ ★ There is no J. Edgar Hoover, but at least twenty-six stand-ins. (1965)

Not true. Art Buchwald published this in his humorous column one day, and some people mistook the joke for fact. This really is more of a misunderstanding than a rumor, as it surely is too farfetched to travel by word of mouth, but one woman was concerned enough about the matter to write to Walter Scott's "Personality Parade," the question-and-answer column that is a regular feature of *Parade* magazine. Mr. Scott has fielded a number of minor rumors over the years ("Is Andy Williams Italian?" "Is Brigitte Bardot secretly taking instruction in the Jewish faith?" "Does Chet Huntley wear a hairpiece?"), along with some wonderful cases of confusion. In October 1982, a woman wrote asking how a man with the responsibilities of Secretary of State George Shultz found time to draw his "Peanuts" cartoon strip. Scott calmly explained that the artist's name was *Charles* Schulz.

★ ★ The Interstate Highway System was built primarily for military reasons. (1960s)

Partly true. Military considerations were an important issue in the debate over funding the massive construction project. At first, in the years just after World War II, the plans called for improvement of existing roadways to adapt them for heavier traffic use. Those arguing for the project claimed that the improved roads would give a boost to interstate commerce and to the economy and that they were necessary for the country's defense, as the military relied on the roads for the movement of troops and equipment. Those arguing against the new road project cited the tremendous expense of the plan.

As the scope of the proposed highway project grew in the early fifties, the arguments for and against remained substantially unchanged—with one exception. After the Russians exploded their first atomic bomb in 1949, the threat of nuclear war made the highway system seem even more important to the country. Now not only the military needed to move quickly in response to the threat of war, but the civilian population of entire cities had to be prepared to evacuate. It is possible that this added danger delivered the votes that ultimately funded the most expensive construction project in our country's history.

★ ★ An industrial city in Japan was renamed "Usa" just after World War II, so that its products could be exported with the imprint "Made in USA." (1950s)

Not true. There is a small town in Japan named Usa, near Kochi on the island of Shikoku, but it was given that name long before World War II, and it is certainly no industrial city. Usa is small enough that it doesn't appear on all maps—we were intrigued at first to find it on a map from 1967 and not on some earlier maps from the fifties—but it has been there all along even though some cartographers overlooked it. Usas can also be found in Russia, Mozambique, and Tanzania. No goods imported from any of the Usas can get by U. S. Customs with a "Made in USA" label. Imported items are required to bear the name of their *country* of origin, not the name of the city or region in which they were made.

★ ★ Swine flu shots were actually vaccinations against a virulent disease that escaped through negligence from a military research laboratory. (1976)

Not true. The nationwide flu vaccination program, which President Ford authorized in March 1976, was launched in reaction to an outbreak of a swine-type flu virus at Fort Dix, New Jersey. The outbreak may have affected as many as five hundred soldiers at the army base, but only four became so sick that they had to rest in bed. One soldier died. That might not seem like enough of an epidemic to justify a national vaccination program, but those who examined the sick soldiers were worried about the similarity between the Fort Dix strain and the strain that had caused the worldwide epidemic of 1918—also thought to have been a swine flu.

The vaccines were developed and mass produced through the spring and summer by three major drug companies, and the first vaccinations were given in Boston on October 1. The plan was to vaccinate a large percentage of the population before the start of the winter flu season, and so prevent a major outbreak. But on October 14, a report appeared in the national press telling of fourteen people who had died within forty-eight hours of receiving the vaccine. Public enthusiasm for the program suddenly vanished. Then came news of people who had been paralyzed with Guillaine-Barre Syndrome as a result of the vaccinations—fifty-four cases. When the vaccination program was prematurely suspended on December 17 because of these suspected dangers, less than a quarter of the population had been vaccinated, not enough to halt an epidemic should the virus have taken hold. The incidence of flu turned out to be unusually light during the winter of 1976–77, even without widespread vaccine protection. There were no outbreaks during 1976 of the diseases the swine flu program was rumored to be concealing—such as bubonic plague and cholera.

In 1983, just when we thought it was safe to get swine flu again, the rumor resurfaced, this time linking the 1976 disease with AIDS. According to the rumor, the government had tried to infect Cuba with its newly developed disease in 1976, but had somehow spread it to Haiti instead. It is now making its way back into the U.S. as AIDS. This, of course, is pure nonsense, an outgrowth of the widespread fear that AIDS has engendered because of its high fatality rate. In fact, AIDS is an extremely rare affliction, equally rare in this country and in Haiti, and it appears not to be easily communicable.

★ ★ The Germans allowed Lenin to travel across Germany from Switzerland to Russia in a "sealed train," hoping he would lead a revolution that would take Russia out of World War I. (1917)

True. This news spread as a rumor long before any verification was possible. The story was told as an example of wartime treachery and later gave credence to a number of false rumors in other conflicts—stories of compliance within Norway that explained the quick German conquest in April 1940, and of the armies of "fifth columnists" that were rumored to be lurking in the United States during World War II waiting for an opportunity to attack from within. Unlike those paranoid fabrications, the story of Lenin's journey through Germany is true.

Lenin, at the time the leader of a small group of extremists, was living in exile in Zurich when in March 1917 the news reached him that revolution had broken out in Russia. After a life of planning to lead such a revolt, he now faced the torment of watching it happen without him. With all of Europe at war, and none of the forces sympathetic to his Bolshevik revolutionaries, there seemed no way of getting back to Russia. But, by indirect negotiation with Germany, carried on through Swiss officials, Lenin was able to strike a deal. The negotiations and arrangements had to be carried out delicately and at arm's length, as Russia was at war with Germany, and as the kaiser ruled just the sort of government that the Bolsheviks sought to overthrow.

The terms of the arrangement made for Lenin stipulated that the kaiser would provide a train to carry a group of exiles through Germany to St. Petersburg, but that during the trip the Russians would have no contact whatsoever with anyone outside the train. In that way the Russians hoped to arrive in St. Petersburg untainted by any possibility of conspiracy with the German enemy. For the kaiser, this was a strategic and devious maneuver. The Bolsheviks had denounced the war as a killer of the working class, and Germany hoped that Lenin would lead his revolutionaries to victory and withdraw Russia from the fray.

Diaries and memoirs of those on the train document the journey, which started in Zurich on April 9, continued through Germany, Sweden, and Finland, and ended in St. Petersburg eight days later with a hero's welcome for Lenin. By November he had become leader of all Russia.

In spite of the careful precautions, Lenin's trip through

Germany did cast suspicions of collusion with the enemy on him, and those suspicions will probably haunt his memory forever. The "sealed train" itself has become a symbol of international treachery. Instead of protecting Lenin's image from stain, it invited comparison of the revolutionaries on the train to a contagion deliberately loosed on Russia by the Germans.

★ ★ A secret underground city exists outside Washington, where key military and government personnel will be whisked in the event of a nuclear war. (1960s)

True. The accidental crash of a TWA jet just outside the fence of the "Mount Weather" relocation center near Upperville, Virginia, in 1974 drew the attention of the press and Congress to a network of such shelters around Washington and to the plans of the Federal Preparedness Agency to save a select group of leaders in order to continue the functions of government even after a massive nuclear attack. Mount Weather turned out to be the primary retreat for the civilian government, while a separate facility called Raven Rock, sixty miles north of Washington, had been built to house military officials.

Some public discussion followed the revelations—congressmen questioned the authority of the Federal Preparedness Agency to choose which aspects of government would survive, and some attacked the policy of allowing those responsible for starting a nuclear war to be the only ones to survive it—but so little information was made public about the relocation plans that the issue quietly died away. Before the silence set in, however, two reporters were able to glean enough information to write a pair of fascinating articles.

Barney Collier, writing for *Harper's Magazine* in 1975, surveyed highly placed Washington officials about the relocation plans and found, among other things, that House Speaker Thomas P. ("Tip") O'Neill was on the list of those to survive, while Senators Harry Byrd and Hubert Humphrey were not. White House Press Secretary Ron Nessen had not been invited, but he vowed to see that his name was added to the list.

Richard Pollock, writing a year later for the *Progressive,* managed to interview several officials who had formerly worked in, or been associated with, the Mount Weather facility. They described the site to Pollock as a pared-down underground city, equipped with streets and sidewalks, restaurants, hospitals, an electric mass-transit system, and even a small lake fed by underground springs.

★ ★ Six students at a college in western Pennsylvania, high on LSD, stared into the sun and blinded themselves. (1967)

Not true. This story was carried on national news-service wires, and quickly wove itself into the fabric of drug mythology in the sixties. It was widely told as a cautionary tale, and widely believed—even by drug users who had grown cynical about such horror stories. It is also one of the few rumors of which we have sure knowledge of the source.

The commissioner of the Office for the Blind of Pennsylvania's Department of Public Welfare fabricated the story in order to impress young people with the dangers of LSD. He made an informal report of the incident to officials in Washington, where it was leaked to the press. Pennsylvania Governor Raymond P. Shafer solemnly confirmed the story at a news conference. But ophthalmologists read the news reports and raised public doubts about the incident. Surely no drug could so completely interfere with the eye-closing reflexes.

An investigation by the attorney general found the commissioner's records to be highly suspect, and in January 1968, he finally broke down, and admitted that the whole thing was a product of his imagination. He was promptly fired from his job, and, deeply disturbed over the incident, he had himself admitted to a psychiatric center.

But, somehow the commissioner's confession didn't make the same splash in the media that the original story had. While he recovered from his ordeal, his story, now known to be a lie, continued to make the rounds. In fact, most people who heard of the incident in the sixties still believe it.

LSD *did* pose dangers to users—and still does. The most serious is the risk of a psychotic break in a person unstable before taking the drug. Many such cases have been documented. In 1967, when use of the drug was spreading rapidly, researchers tried desperately to find out what possible side effects LSD might have. Since there was not time for long-term studies, they often had to settle for less-conclusive evidence, and the press often made more of tentative study results than the actual studies warranted. The discovery of broken chromosomes in the blood cells of some heavy LSD users led researchers to speculate on the possibility of long-term genetic damage from the drug. This led to reports of birth defects well before any such cases had been found. The *Saturday Evening Post* printed an article in 1967 about an Oregon child born with defective intestines and a head that was "developing grotesquely—one side growing at a much faster rate than the other." A check by *Time* magazine revealed that the infant was in fact normal in all respects. Other LSD-related birth defects were reported periodically in the press, and LSD users came to believe that that was one of the inevitable side effects of the drug, but all such reports were based on rumor. There have, of course, been defective children born to parents who used LSD, but no statistical correlation has ever developed.

★ ★ Ritz crackers have the word "sex" embossed on them to make them more subliminally attractive to buyers. (1960s)

Not true. We have studied quite a few Ritz crackers in the course of our research—sometimes with cheese on them, sometimes with peanut butter, and sometimes plain—and we have *never* come across that offending word.

There have been several serious studies made of the use of subliminal devices in advertising, among them Wilson Bryan Key's book *Subliminal Seduction*. Key shows case after case of supposedly deliberate attempts by advertisers to reach our subconscious—through sexual imagery in the ice cubes in liquor ads, through the use of ancient and archetypal symbols, and in many other ways. We remained singularly unconvinced after reading the book, but the subject cannot be dismissed on the basis of our judgment alone.

Most of us have heard that movie theaters boost their sales of refreshments by flashing one-frame messages on the screen during a film. It is said that you can tell this has happened to you when you suddenly get an urge for some refreshment in the middle of the movie, and, as you get up to go out in the lobby, you notice thirty other people doing the same thing. In 1956, marketing researcher James Vicary did test such subliminal advertising in a crude experiment at a Fort Lee, New Jersey movie theater. For six weeks he flashed brief (1/3000-second) messages on the theater screen reading "Hungry? Eat popcorn" and "Drink Coca-Cola." Vicary reported that popcorn sales swelled by 57.8 percent, and Coca-Cola sales by 18 percent. But since he didn't establish a control for his experiment, the results are virtually meaningless. They may as easily have been caused by seasonal variation in attendance and snack preference as by Vicary's subliminal messages. The public outcry over the experiment effectively shut down that fledgling branch of the advertising industry. Both the National Association of Broadcasters and the Federal Communications Commission now explicitly bar the use of such subliminal advertising techniques.

If you're interested in seeing a non-commercial example of a subliminal flash, pay close attention the next time you see Alfred Hitchcock's film *Psycho* (1960). In the very last shot of the movie the camera focuses on Anthony Perkins's face, which suddenly looks exceedingly gruesome. The reason: a single-frame flash of a human skull.

Some Christian extremists claim that the recordings of certain rock groups contain hidden Satanic messages, which, like the movie flashes, can only be discerned by our subconscious minds. The messages can supposedly be heard clearly if the records are played backward. William Poundstone, in his admirably-researched book *Big Secrets*, rented a recording studio to get to the bottom of these accusations. He found most of them groundless, but he did make some interesting discoveries. Led Zeppelin's song "Stairway to Heaven" does yield a coherent phrase, "There's no escape," when played in reverse, and, later in the song, the word "Satan." Both matched up to much clearer forward-playing lyrics, and can only have been produced in reverse by accident. Poundstone also found some intentionally reversed messages. At the beginning of the song "Empty Spaces" on Pink Floyd's album

"The Wall," an unintelligible voice can be heard. In reverse, the voice becomes completely coherent, saying, "Congratulations, you have just discovered the secret message. . . ." Electric Light Orchestra worked a reversed message into their song "Fire On High." Again, the voice makes no sense when played normally, but in reverse says, "The music is reversible, but time—turn back! Turn back! Turn back! Turn back!"

We have also heard that Muzak transmits subliminal messages—either to work harder or to buy more, depending on where the music is played. Muzak has been proven to increase work output and up sales by making people more comfortable and happy with its soothing sounds, but that is as far as its subliminal influence goes. Or so we thought until, one frazzled day, we were put on hold during a telephone call and the receptionist flipped on a calming Muzak version of "I Will Wait For You If It Takes Forever." We ended up waiting forever. Maybe there is something to this after all.

★ ★ Procter & Gamble is run by devil worshipers. (1982)

Not true. According to the most rampant version of this rumor, a high executive of Procter & Gamble appeared on the Merv Griffin show (or Phil Donahue, "20/20", or "60 Minutes") and made the stunning admission that his company was run by devil worshipers and that the corporation donated ten percent of its income to satanic groups. As further proof, the rumormongers pointed to the thirteen stars on the company's trademark and to the fact that these connect to form three sixes—*666* being one of the devil's favorite numbers. The rumor was most deeply entrenched in the South, where it was preached as fact from the pulpits of several fundamentalist churches.

This rumor is a revival, of sorts, of a milder and less troublesome rumor that Procter & Gamble weathered in 1980—that the company was owned by the Unification Church of the Reverend Sun Myung Moon—more commonly known as the "Moonies." This rumor undoubtedly had its basis in the company's symbol as well.

The company survived the first rumor without too much trouble, but the story about the devil worshipers was more tenacious. In June 1982, calls to the company's toll-free number asking about the rumor reached the level of six hundred a day. That summer Procter & Gamble decided to fight the rumor; by waiting quietly, they seemed to be letting the falsehood run out of control.

The company pressed charges against several southern ministers for spreading the story. It launched an extensive advertising campaign to deny the rumor, and company spokespersons explained the *real* history of the man-in-the-moon trademark to the media (the thirteen stars were probably a patriotic gesture when the logo was drawn in 1882). In addition, religious leaders like Jerry Falwell and Billy Graham were asked to help in the effort to quash the rumor.

The story has quieted down, whether as a result of the company's efforts or because it simply ran its course. If it showed us nothing else, the rumor certainly shed a revealing light on a part of America we rarely think of: a lot of people believe strongly enough in the existence of the devil to think that a major corporation could be under his direct control. Procter & Gamble received fifteen thousand telephone calls in one month from the easily persuaded.

Earlier versions of the Procter & Gamble trademark, showing its evolution

★ ★ There was once a woman Pope.

Not true. One of the enduring myths about the Catholic church, in circulation since the eleventh century, holds that a mysterious Pope John VIII (854–856) was actually a woman. He/she is known to believers of this story as Pope Joan, and a dense body of biographical detail has been supplied for her over the centuries.

The daughter of a British missionary to the Saxons, she entered the sisterhood after the death of her parents, and she fell in love with a monk. In order to continue the romance without incurring punishment, Joan donned the robes of a monk herself, and, from then until she died, she impersonated a man. By diligent study and artful political maneuvering, she found herself in Rome as a religious teacher, then as secretary to Pope Pius IV, and, on his death, as the pope herself. But she was undone by her own lack of restraint. She became pregnant by her bodyguard (or perhaps a cardinal), and gave birth in front of an astonished crowd while delivering a litany. The angry flock responded by beating her and the infant to death. In some versions of the tale, the infant survived, spirited away by the forces of the devil, and is still alive, waiting to fulfill his role as the anti-Christ in the final days of the world.

Medieval as this story sounds, and, despite its complete lack of historical foundation, it still has its adherents. Though it seems incredible, there are to this day people who believe in plots by devil worshipers to conceal the anti-Christ. Consider the 1967 book *Rosemary's Baby* and remember how easy it was for yourself to imagine such a plot. And consider a 1982 rumor almost as wild as the one about Pope Joan: that Pope John Paul II is the anti-Christ, appointed through

Soviet influence; his actions will lead to the start of World War III.

★ ★ In 1960, when Pope John XXIII read the secret message of Our Lady of Fatima, which had been kept until then in a sealed envelope, he cried for three days over the terrible news it revealed, but he never discussed what he had read. (1960)

Unconfirmed. When three shepherd children in Fatima, Portugal, were visited several times by a vision of the Virgin Mary in 1917, she left them with several predictions and a warning to make public. These included a vision of hell; a prediction that World War I would soon end and that another still more terrible war would start under the next supreme pontiff (Pope Pius XI, 1922–39); and a warning that, if Russia did not consecrate itself to her, it would "spread its errors throughout the world," causing many countries to be "annihilated." A final detail of the prediction was to be kept secret until a later date, and it is this part of the vision that has given rise to rumor and speculation. All that the children would say of this last prediction at the time was that it would bring joy to some and sorrow to others.

Two of the children died of influenza soon after the war, as the vision had predicted they would, and the surviving witness, Lucia Santos, became a nun. Between 1935 and 1941 she wrote four volumes of memoirs describing her visions. As part of this work, she put on paper the last and secret prediction and sealed it in an envelope with instructions that

147

it be opened no later than 1960, or upon her death. In 1957, according to a church source, the envelope still lay sealed in the office of the Bishop of Leiria in Portugal. The church has not revealed its contents or given any information as to whether the letter has yet been opened. Lucia Santos is still alive in a Carmelite convent in Spain and has taken a new name: Sister Maria of the Immaculate Heart.

The three Seers of Fatima: Jacinta, Francis, and Lucia

★ ★ There are full-grown alligators in the sewers of New York City. They were pets brought back from vacations in Florida, then flushed down toilets when their owners grew tired of keeping them. (1960s)

Possibly true. This is one of the most widely circulated rumors we have encountered. Just about everyone we have asked in the course of our research knew this one, though almost everyone doubted it could be true. Well, we have news for you. It just might *be* true. Or at least it may have been true for a time in the 1930s.

Between 1932 and 1938 the *New York Times* printed several reports of alligators caught around the city—in the Bronx River, in New Jersey, in the East River, and even in a Brooklyn subway station. On August 16, 1938, the paper told of a sudden bonanza in alligator fishing in Huguenot Lake in New Rochelle, just to the north of the city. Five of the reptiles had been caught by fishermen over the weekend. Major Elvin L. Barr managed to land two, using ordinary bass flies. He theorized that the creatures "had been put there by some resident who had bought them in Florida as pets and then tired of them." Did we see those wondering eyebrows go up? But wait. A story even more crucial to the rumor appeared on February 10, 1935, under the headline "Alligator Found in Uptown Sewer." According to the *Times* reporter, several boys on East 123rd Street were shoveling snow into a manhole when they spotted an alligator in the sewer below. They lassoed it with a clothesline and dragged it out onto the street, where it was found to be "seven and a half or eight feet" long. The story is so important to the analysis of this rumor that we include it here in full. We'll let you read it and draw your own conclusions.

ALLIGATOR FOUND IN UPTOWN SEWER

Youths Shoveling Snow Into
Manhole See the Animal
Churning in Icy Water.

SNARE IT AND DRAG IT OUT

Reptile Slain by Rescuers When
It Gets Vicious—Whence It
Came Is Mystery.

The youthful residents of East 123d Street, near the murky Harlem River, were having a rather grand time at dusk yesterday shoveling the last of the recent snow into a gaping manhole.

Salvatore Condulucci, 16 years old, of 419 East 123d Street, was assigned to the rim. His comrades would heap blackened slush near him, and he, carefully observing the sewer's capacity, would give the last fine flick to each mound.

Suddenly there were signs of clogging ten feet below, where the manhole drop merged with the dark conduit leading to the river. Salvatore yelled: "Hey, you guys, wait a minute," and got down on his knees to see what was the trouble.

What he saw, in the thickening dusk, almost caused him to topple into the icy cavern. For the jagged surface of the ice blockade below was moving; and something black was breaking through. Salvatore's eyes widened; then he managed to leap to his feet and call his friends.

"Honest, it's an alligator!" he exploded.

Others Look and Are Convinced.

There was a murmur of skepticism. Jimmy Mireno, 19, of 440 East 123d Street, shouldered his way to the rim and stared.

"He's right," he said.

Frank Lonzo, 18, of 1,743 Park Avenue, looked next. He also confirmed the spectre. Then there was a great crush about the opening in the middle of the street and heads were bent low around the aperture.

The animal apparently was threshing about in the ice, trying to get clear. When the first wave of awe had passed, the boys decided to help it out. A delegation was dispatched to the Lehigh Stove and Repair Shop at 441 East 123d Street.

"We want some clothes-line," demanded the delegation, and got it.

Young Condulucci, an expert on Western movies, fashioned a slip knot. With the others watching breathlessly, he dangled the noose into the sewer, and after several tantalizing near-catches, looped it about the 'gator's neck. Then he pulled hard. There was a grating of rough leathery skin against jumbled ice. But the job was too much for one youth. The others grabbed the rope and all pulled.

Slowly, with its curving tail twisting weakly, the animal was dragged from the snow, ten feet through the dank cavern, and to the street, where it lay, non-committal; it was not in Florida, that was clear.

And therefore, when one of the boys sought to loosen the rope, the creature opened its jaws and snapped, not with the robust vigor of a healthy, well-sunned alligator, but with the

150

fury of a sick, very badly treated one. The boys jumped back. Curiosity and sympathy turned to enmity.

"Let 'im have it" the cry went up.

Rescuers Then Kill it.

So the shovels that had been used to pile snow on the alligator's head were now to rain blows upon it. The 'gator's tail swished about a few last times. Its jaws clashed weakly. But it was in no mood for a real struggle after its icy incarceration. It died on the spot.

Triumphantly, but not without the inevitable reaction of sorrow, the boys took their victim to the Lehigh Stove and Repair Shop. There it was found to weigh 125 pounds; they said it measured seven and a half or eight feet. It became at once the greatest attraction the store ever had had. The whole neighborhood milled about, and finally, a call for the police reached a nearby station.

But there was little for the hurrying policemen to do. The strange visitor was quite dead; and no charge could be preferred against it or against its slayers. The neighbors were calmed with little trouble and speculation as to where the 'gator had come from was rife.

There are no pet shops in the vicinity; that theory was ruled out almost at once. Finally, the theories simmered down to that of a passing boat. Plainly, a steamer from the mysterious Everglades, or thereabouts, had been passing 123d Street, and the alligator had fallen overboard.

Shunning the hatefully cold water, it had swum toward shore and found only the entrance to the conduit. Then after another 150 yards through a torrent of melting snow—and by that time it was half dead—it had arrived under the open manhole.

Half-dead, yes, the neighborhood conceded. But still alive enough for a last splendid opening and snapping of its jaws. The boys were ready to swear to that.

At about 9 P. M., when tired mothers had succeeded in getting most of their alligator-conscious youngsters to bed, a Department of Sanitation truck rumbled up to the store and made off with the prize. Its destination was Barren Island and an incinerator.

The newspaper reports give evidence that in the thirties there may have been a factual basis for the rumor. But they don't explain how the rumor suddenly became so popular in the sixties. For that we have to turn to a book published in 1959—Robert R. Daley's *The World Beneath the City.*

Daley, a sports reporter for the *New York Times,* devoted a whole chapter in his book to alligators in the New York City sewers. He tells how Sewer Superintendent Teddy May first started hearing reports of alligators from his inspectors in 1935. He responded by sending a couple of assistants down to find out how the sewer walkers were managing to smuggle whiskey in with them to work. The agents reported that there seemed to be no drinking going on, but that the men were still seeing alligators. May decided to investigate the matter himself. After a few hours down below, he was convinced. With his own eyes he had seen a number of the beasts, of an average length of about two feet.

According to Daley, Superintendent May then launched a campaign to clean the animals out of the sewers. Some of the reptiles were killed with rat poison. Others were flushed out of the slow-moving backwaters into the swift current of the main pipes, which swept them out to sea. Some drowned when the pipes they were hiding in flooded to the top. And some were hunted down by sewer workers with guns. By 1936 all the alligators were gone. Or so claims Robert Daley.

He theorizes that the reptiles got into the sewers by being dropped into storm drains and manholes when owners grew tired of keeping them as pets. That makes a little more sense than the toilet route, since many of the creatures must have grown somewhat during their tenure as pets—and a two-foot alligator could clog a toilet pretty seriously. But what makes Daley think that people stopped dropping pets into manholes in 1935? Surely some of the alligators that came up from Florida through the forties would have received the same treatment as the earlier pets. We wonder.

Daley's book was widely reviewed in 1959 and 1960, and the reviews often referred to the alligator chapter. It was probably these mentions, rather than the book itself, that revived the rumor—since the book was not nearly as widely read as the newspapers and magazines that reviewed it. Daley also wrote an article for the *New York Times Magazine* in 1958. In it he gave an abbreviated account of the story—

he told how the animals grew to "alarming" sizes in the sewers, but he didn't mention that they had been eliminated.

Thomas Pynchon worked the alligators-in-the-sewers legend into his 1963 novel *V* and incorporated in his fiction some details that the rumor has picked up in the process of its maturation—that the creatures have turned blind and albino from their life of darkness, and that they grow to monstrous size on their diet of rats. (In the 1980 film *Alligator,* one grew *really* big when chemical waste was flushed into his sewer.) Since then a companion story has grown up. Now the alligators live among huge marijuana plants, sprouted from seeds flushed down toilets during drug raids. The plants, like the alligators, are albino, and the smoke they produce is extraordinarily potent. Dealers sell the variety as "New York City White." We know of no factual basis for this story.

We'll leave you with the opinion of an expert. In May 1982, the *New York Times* quoted John Flaherty, Chief of Design for the New York City Bureau of Sewers, as stating that "there are no alligators in the New York City sewer system." We don't believe him. Do you?

Acknowledgments

WE WOULD NOT HAVE BEEN ABLE to write this book without the help of numerous friends, rumormongers, and experts. For their editorial guidance and other help, our appreciation to Gerry Howard, Rick Balkin, and Polly Cone; for providing special research on strange subjects, our thanks to Ken Boege, Richard Tucker, and John Neyenesch; and to our most productive rumor source, Richard Maurer, our deepest respect. Thanks also to Reg Abbiss at Rolls-Royce Motors, L. L. Ulrey and Bruce Verskin at Procter & Gamble, Corky Brown at Dr. Pepper, Isabelle Avrutov at Revlon, David R. Smith at Walt Disney Archives, Elaine Viets at the *St. Louis Post-Dispatch*, Leon Rosenman, Susan Marsh, Sig Roos, Ellen Morgan, Diane McCaffrey, Diane Dunne, Bill Farragher, Jeff Stone, Bob Pfeiffer, Don Tucker, Betty Tucker, Henry Morgan, Gwen Morgan, Richard Kusleika, Fred Baca, Phil Grabar, Larra Andress, Sonya Kittrell, A. Dertouzos, Lance LeVine, Diane Sutor, Lynde Kelley, Damian Kravets, Tammy Smith, Joseph Albanese, Denise Binkley, Rick Rader, Jeffrey Kroessler, Lisa Stanley, Robin Neal, Mark A. Zeiger, Patricia Tyl, Glenda Boyd, Martha Weil, Maureen Serb, Tracy Bruce, Dee Tatum England, Steve Moore, Lynn Zipfel Venhaus, John Chappell, Jonathan Chamberlain, Steve Terrell, Brenda Crews, Mrs. Fenton R. Talbot, Susan Behrens, Beverly Johnson Such, Beverly Cobb, David L. Swierat, Peter Boorman, Lyn Connery, George Hadley-Garcia, Jonathan Bravard, Sarah Rushton, Alex Trullinger, Stephanie Samuels, John L. Yarbo, Jr., Kathy O'Connell, Brad Daggett and Dan Grinko.

INDEX

REQUEST FOR RUMORS

WE ARE CONTINUING our rumor research, and would appreciate any help that you can give us. If you hear or remember any interesting rumors that we haven't discussed, please send us a note. It would be helpful if you let us know the year in which you first heard each rumor—as closely as you can remember. We'll acknowledge all letters that include a return address.

We will share your letters with other rumor and folklore researchers, and we'll draw on them if we do a sequel to this book.

Please address your correspondence to us at:

Steam Press
P.O. Box 16
Cambridge, MA 02140